Come Undone

Club Silken, Volume 4

Jerrie Alexander

Published by Jerrie Alexander, 2024.

Club Silken

Jerrie Alexander

Published in the United States of America

This series is intended for mature audiences only due to sexual situations, explicit language, and some BDSM.

Acknowledgments

Kym Roberts, thank you for being my friend. I am truly blessed. Although most of our conversations and brainstorming sessions are best not repeated, I appreciate how we develop some interesting plotlines together. I only wish my brain worked as fast as yours.

My Beta readers, thank you isn't a strong enough word. You totally rock. I'm so lucky to have your support and honesty. You are truly dear friends. You stuck with me through the years of darkness, believed in me, and I appreciate each of you.

Eve Arroyo, editor extraordinaire, I love your honesty and brilliant mind. You always ask the right questions, putting me back on point when the story stumbles.

Brynna Curry, how do I thank you? You're beautiful covers lift my spirits. You've become a huge part of my writing life and as a friend. If you weren't around to hold up both ends of the ship when I falter, I don't know what I'd do. Thank you!

Prologue

Come Undone

Kenzie

"No. No. No. Not now." I'm yelling at a dying car but, of course, it's not helping. After a series of sputters, shudders, and coughs, my eleven-year-old car, which has been a loyal friend, dies.

Steering to the side of the road is good in theory, but without the engine running, there's no power steering. My arm muscles scream in protest while I put every ounce of strength I have into coasting this baby onto the shoulder of the road. When I finally stop rolling, I put on the emergency brake, turn on my flashers, unhook my seat belt, and hop out.

A truck zips past and the driver honks at me, causing me to just about jump out of my skin. I think about flipping him off, but I don't. Technically, the ass end of my car is off the road. You can call it barely, but in this case, barely counts. It's not like I'm blocking a lane. I pop the hood and raise it, not sure what I'm looking at or for, but I stare at the steam rising into the air for a minute.

My options are few. There's not much in the way of businesses on this highway full of speeding drivers, all with somewhere they need to be.

Sweat breaks and runs between my boobs, soaking the band of my bra and reminding me it's July and Chicago is in the middle of a heatwave. I pull out my cell and stare at it as if the name and phone number of someone who will help me will magically appear. It's five o'clock on a Friday, and the few people I know don't own a car or are on the highway headed home from work.

Work. *Crap.* My stomach clenches. Tonight is one of the busiest nights of the weekend for the steak house where I work. Not only am I going to leave them shorthanded, but I'll also miss out on my wages plus some desperately needed tips.

The deep rumble of a motorcycle drowns out my thoughts. The man stops, kills the engine, and uses one of the big black boots he's wearing to drop the kickstand. He slings a leg over the tank, gets off, and removes his helmet. His hand shoves long stringy hair off his face as he stalks toward me.

I read romance books and the bikers are macho, sexy as hell, and they save the damsel in distress. This guy sends the wrong kind of chills up my spine. The wife-beater he's wearing was probably white at one time, and his jeans could use a thorough washing.

"Looks like you need a little help." His eyes slide over my face, stopping at my boobs. "Those long legs will wrap around my. . ."

My eyebrows shoot toward my hairline.

"They'll fit around my bike just fine."

He must not understand the meaning of personal space because he just keeps coming toward me. I step back, only to find myself between him and my dead car. The smell of alcohol and unwashed body parts reaches me before he does. "I appreciate you stopping, but a friend is coming to pick me up. Thanks anyway."

He ignores my subtle dismissal and steps closer. "Bullshit. No need for you to wait. I'll take you anywhere you want to go. Maybe we'll stop for a drink on the way."

"No really. My boyfriend will be here in a few minutes."

Biker Guy sways, looking unsteady on his feet. I'm thinking I can outrun him, but where will I go? Cars are flying down the highway, and nobody is paying attention to us.

His eyes narrow. "He ain't much of a boyfriend letting you drive that broken-down piece of shit."

"It has sentimental value." I can't vouch for the first five years of her existence, but she's been a good ride for the past six.

I tap the nine on my phone to call for help but pause when a shiny silver Corvette pulls over and stops. The door opens and a man steps out. He's wearing slacks and a white shirt. "There he is," I say with a grin plastered on my face.

I scoot around Biker Guy and run to the good Samaritan walking toward us. I don't give him a chance to speak. I wrap my arms around him and give him a big hug.

"Honey." I look up into his face, talking loudly enough to get over the low din of the highway. "I'm glad you finally got here."

Amusement flits across the guy's face, and his mouth curves into a half-smile. All my words vanish. Heat shoots up my face, and I release him as if my hair is on fire. My fingers itch, and I clasp them together to keep them from unbuttoning his shirt and checking for a giant red S on his undershirt. Okay, I know he's not Clark Kent but holy shit.

Probably in his early thirties, the man has a tall frame with broad shoulders, black hair, and eyes the color of the Caribbean Sea. The tailored shirt he's wearing fits like a glove. He steps back, tilts his head, and looks down at me. At this point, he knows I'm staring.

His gaze sweeps the scene in front of him, no doubt trying to understand the situation he's gotten himself into. His arm slides around my waist and tugs me closer. I have to tilt my head back to look up at him, and that doesn't happen often. "I got here as fast as I could. Let's take a look at your car."

I nod my response as another run of sweat slides down my chest. I issue a silent prayer that I don't smell like Biker Guy after standing out here in the sun. 'Vette Guy's arm guides me over to my car. He nods and smiles at Biker Guy.

"Thanks for stopping to help my girl. Looks like no one else was willing to take the time. I appreciate it."

"You're her man and you drive a fucking 'Vette, while your woman drives a piece of shit?"

Unfazed, 'Vette Guy nods. "True, but what she drives isn't your concern, is it?" He lowers the hood on my car and turns to me. "I'll have it towed to a garage."

These two bulls are staring each other down, and male testosterone is getting thicker by the second. So, I kiss 'Vette Guy on the cheek. The disruptive tactic works and both men look at me like I'd just landed from Mars.

"Honey, we need to get going." I look up at him with adoring eyes.

"Me too. I've got business to take care of." Biker Guy climbs aboard his bike, and within seconds, it roars to life. He revs the engine and rides off, slinging dirt and gravel from under his tires. I swear the ground shakes under my feet.

"Thank you." I wave my hand in front of my face to clear the air. Reluctantly, I remove myself from 'Vette Guy's arm and take my cell out. "I appreciate you stopping. I'll be okay now. You don't have to wait with me."

"Really? You're dismissing me so quickly?" He flashes straight white teeth at me. "After all we've been through?"

"I'm afraid so."

"Are you calling family?"

My spine automatically stiffens. "No," I snap. "I truly am grateful you stopped since it could have gotten ugly, but I'm fine now. Okay?"

"No. It's not okay. I'm not leaving you out here for easy-picking. Remember the asshole who just left? There's more where he came from." The timbre of Samaritan Guy's voice tells me his mind is made up. "I'm happy to take you wherever you were headed."

"I don't know you. Granted, you smell better than he did, but you could be a serial killer for all I know. Thank you for stopping, but I can take care of myself."

"Justin Locke. Pleased to meet you." He blows out a huff of air as if I've offended him. Before I can react, my cell is in his hand. He snaps a picture of his license plate, takes a selfie, and texts himself. "Send those pictures to whoever you were going to call and tell them if you're not in touch within the hour to call the cops."

Damn. He's good. And the battle of "should I stay or should I go" is off and running in my head.

"Not enough?" He pulls his wallet from his hip pocket, removes his driver's license, and takes a shot of it too before handing my cell back to me. "Now, will you get in the car?"

"Bossy much?"

A chuckle rolls from somewhere deep inside him, and one corner of his mouth kicks up into a grin. "You have no idea."

My knees are suddenly weak. If circumstances were different, I wouldn't mind taking an order or two from him. I have no doubt he gets what he wants.

"You're as safe with me as I am with you." He walks to his car and opens the passenger side door for me.

I grab my purse from my car and my uniform that's hanging in the back. The furrow between his brows deepens when I close the door on my car, pat the roof, say goodbye, and join him.

"Did you just talk to an inanimate object?"

"I did. You have a problem with that?"

"Not even one." He's looking at me as if I've escaped a madhouse.

"That car and I have been through a lot together." I have no idea why I'm defending my behavior. Yes, I do. He's too pushy.

"In."

He catches my elbow, and I allow him to steady me as I lower all five foot eight inches of my body into his car. His is one of those automobiles that sit inches above the ground, causing my entrance to be less than graceful. How any woman wearing a dress can get in or out of this car without flashing the world is a mystery. One I won't have to solve.

He closes the door, walks around, and slides in behind the steering wheel. A second later, the 'Vette rumbles to life, reminding me of a big cat purring. A huge, angry cat.

"Where to?"

I extend my right hand. "Since we both could be in danger, we should probably know each other's names. I'm Kenzie Stone."

"As I said before, Justin Locke." He rewards me with another of his half-smiles as his hand swallows mine. His grip is strong, and I have this urge not to give him his hand back. "Where to?" he asks again.

I consider having him drop me off at work, but instead, I give him the address of my apartment complex. I'm too anxious to carry around trays of food while I'm trying to figure out how I'm going to pay for a tow and repairs. He taps in the information with long thick fingers. He drives into traffic and quickly navigates to the fast lane.

"Thank you."

"You're welcome. My grandfather would spin in his grave if I ignored a woman stranded anywhere. Much less a beautiful woman."

I ignore that last part. I know what I look like with my hair tied back and makeup at a minimum. It's not beautiful. "He must have been a good man."

"He was."

We ride in the uncomfortable silence of two total strangers for a few minutes. I decide to ask questions. "What do you do for a living?"

"I'm the owner and CEO of a major systems design company."

"So, you are off work for the weekend, and I shouldn't feel too guilty about keeping you from being somewhere, right?"

"Close but not one hundred percent accurate. I'm also co-owner of an adults only club and tonight's the grand opening."

My brain stops at the words *adults only*. "Somehow, I don't think you're referring to a country club, are you?"

"No. It's a place where people who live a certain lifestyle can be comfortable, and no one passes judgment."

"A sex club?" The ride just got a lot more interesting.

"Exactly." He glances at me. "Did I detect a note of curiosity in your question?"

"You did not." He's gorgeous, has money, and is way out of my league. That doesn't stop me from wondering how his hands would feel on my naked body after he handcuffed me.

"Sounded like it to me." He needs to stop glancing over at me with that sexy half-grin. "How much do you know about BDSM?"

My jaw comes unhinged. Is he reading my mind? "I read."

"In other words, nothing." He changes lanes, accelerates, and speeds past a slower-moving car.

"I admit you're right. My knowledge of the subject is limited to books."

"You shouldn't rely on romance novels for information. If you're the least bit curious, it's best to see it firsthand."

My brain shifts into overload, and the blood in my veins heat at the thought of what he means by *firsthand*. I've read lots of books that were written around BDSM, mafia bosses, and men who dominate women in general. The stories serve as a constant reminder I don't have time for a sex life. I've just about forgotten what having an orgasm feels like. Well, one that's not self-induced.

"If that's an invitation, no thanks. Between work and college, sex isn't my top priority."

"What are you studying that you can't take time out for sex?"

"I'm going to be a paralegal when I grow up. If I stay the course, which I will, I'll take the exam with the Association for Legal Professionals in January on my twenty-fifth birthday."

"Good for you." He reaches over and pats my knee. "If my first impression of you is right, you'll succeed."

"Thanks."

"You snapped at me when I mentioned family. You're not close?"

"I might be if I had any."

"Living without family must be tough." He glances at me when I don't respond. "Do you have someone to help with your car?"

"I do." I try to sound like I'm telling the truth.

"Really?" He guides the car to the outside lane, shoots down the ramp, and off the freeway. A couple of blocks later, he's driving through the gate and stopping in front of my apartment building. "Who's going to help?"

"Thank you so much. I'll pay it forward." I unbuckle, grab my stuff, and hop out, avoiding his question.

"It was my pleasure. Take care of yourself."

I close the car door and hurry inside. I don't understand the effect he had on me, but my heart hasn't stopped racing since I gave him the fake kiss. I hate to see him drive away, out of my life forever. I stop, turn just inside the stairwell, and watch until his sports car is out of sight. I jog up the stairs, smiling. Not many women can say a superhero saved them.

I call work and explain my situation to the manager. He asks if I can work tomorrow, which is my day off, and I jump on that. It will help pay for using the bus system since the train doesn't run this route. My stomach rolls into a knot. I didn't consider how much my car repair is going to set me back. I'll have to dip into what little savings I have. If that doesn't cover the cost, the balance has to go on my credit card.

I spend a few minutes on Google trying to find a company to tow my car to a repair shop. I decide to wait until I get to work tomorrow. One of my coworkers will know who I need to contact. I fix a sandwich, slip on a pair of sleep shorts and a T-shirt, and spread my homework out across my bed.

***

My alarm jars me awake, I discover my laptop still on, and my head is resting on an open book. I haven't accomplished nearly as much as I planned. Rolling out of bed, I save what little work I completed and go to the kitchen. The restaurant doesn't serve breakfast, so I have a few hours to kill. I fix myself a cup of coffee and start my weekend routine of washing clothes and getting ready for the upcoming week.

It's after lunch before I shower and dress in shorts and a tank top. I finally have time to work on my unfinished homework, so I grab my laptop, open my balcony door, and sit at the small round table in the corner. My view is of the parking lot, but I'm good with that for now. Someday I'll have a job that pays enough for a larger apartment.

It's hot again today, and the sun feels good on my skin. The urge to slip on my bathing suit and hit the pool is strong, but the need to finish this assignment is stronger. I stand to refill my cup and notice a beige Ford pulling into the parking lot. It's exactly like mine. I walk to the iron railing and watch my car as it's driven into an empty slot right in front of the entrance to the building.

I'm barefoot but that doesn't stop me from racing through my living room, down the stairs, and outside. I arrive just in time to watch a second car pull away. I assume with the driver of my car. The pavement is hot beneath my feet, but I can't turn back. I run the rest of the way, open the door, and get inside.

It takes a second before I realize I left my car on the side of the road with the key in the ignition. I start my poor old friend, and she hums to life. I turn off the engine and just sit here in the heat. My superhero had her towed and repaired.

Justin's kindness overwhelms me. I don't know how to react. How to feel. I've taken care of myself since I was six years old. People don't do things for me unless there's something in it for them. Tears fill my eyes and spill down my cheeks. I think back to the last time I cried. It was the day I accepted my mother was never coming to get me.

I spot a white envelope on the passenger seat. I pick it up and carefully open it. Inside is an embossed invitation to Club Satin to be used in seven months on my twenty-fifth birthday. The only instruction is to ask for Slider.

"Who is Slider?" I ask out loud.

Chapter 1

Slider

Seven months later

"It's a full house," Danielle says, closing the door to my office behind her.

"Great." I scan the monitors, roll my chair away from my desk, and turn toward her. "Thanks for working through the waiting list for membership. I emailed the names to Gabriel for background checks."

Mentally and physically, the manager of this club is star quality. Trained at our first adult's only club, Silken, which Zack Pierce and Nick Bianco opened, Danielle Moore is a huge asset to Satin. Dark red hair, a hot body, and a mind like a steel trap, she runs this place like a fine-tuned Swiss watch. Not one detail slips past her. She brings a lot to the table.

"Nick and Kayla just arrived. Their demonstration isn't for an hour, so I seated them in their usual booth."

"Good." I nod my approval. "I'll be out in a few minutes."

"But that's not why I came in here."

"Okay. What's up?"

"There's a woman at the front desk asking for Slider. Are you expecting anyone?"

"No, but if she's a member, send her back."

"She's not."

"Tell her I'm not available." Training a sub and then matching her up with the perfect Dom is something I used to enjoy but don't have time for any longer.

"She has an invitation. One of the embossed originals."

"Those only went out to couples." The hair on the back of my neck stands. It has to be the bearer of the only single invitation I've ever given out. It has to be the girl from the side of the road. "Except for one I personally gave out."

"She's a strawberry blond with long wavy hair pulled back on the sides and legs that go on forever. If you don't want her, I do."

I laugh at her offer. "If it's who I think it is, she's off-limits. In fact, she doesn't belong here."

"Oh?" Danielle's eyes are full of curiosity. "Should I turn her away?"

"No." I stand and follow Danielle out of my office, slowing down to say hello to a few members at the bar while making my way to the entrance of the club.

I enter the foyer and look around. Gabriel and one of his men shake their heads. "She just left."

I push open the outer doors and step into the night just in time to see the light inside her car come on. By the time I reach her, she's buckled up, ready to drive away. I stop between the headlights and place my hands on the hood.

She kills the ignition, unhooks, and gets out. "I decided you didn't remember me."

"Impatient much?" I struggle to keep my jaw in place as she walks toward me. Her long legs are bare under a black pencil skirt, and a cream sweater half covers the white blouse she's wearing. The heels on her shoes put her just above chin level with me.

"You have no idea."

"Touché." I'm flattered she remembers part of our conversation from so long ago. She smiles, and my dick comes to life, twitching its approval. "I'm sorry you had to wait. I see you're still driving the same car."

"Thanks to the TLC you gave her, she drives like a new one."

"She? You think a car has an identifiable sex?" This woman is gorgeous. I must've been too wrapped up in getting the club open to notice her creamy complexion and deep blue eyes.

"Of course, they do." Her eyes sparkle under the parking lot lights. A gust of wind sends a shiver over her. "At least this one does." She chuckles at her joke, and my brain absorbs the sound.

I could get addicted to that laugh. No doubt, her cry of release will be even more addictive. Is she interested in being my sub? Not a trainee, my personal submissive. Is she the kind of woman who will drop to her knees on command? I certainly want to find out.

"Come inside, out of the cold. I'll buy you a drink."

"No, thanks." She turns away, reaches inside her car, and pulls out an envelope. Walking around to the front of her car, she offers it to me. "I only came to bring this to you."

"What is it?"

"Reimbursement for having my car hauled and repaired."

"What?" I take a step back. "It was nothing."

"It was huge, and you know it."

"If we're going to argue, can we go inside out of the weather?" I wave toward the front door of Satin. "Please. Join me. We can go to my office."

Her chin lifts and she holds the envelope out to me. "This is for you."

"I'm not taking your money. I don't need to be reimbursed for doing the right thing." That she feels compelled to pay me back is important to her. I like that, as young as she is, she has a sense of responsibility. "But I'll give you a chance to change my mind."

After a long pause, she nods and closes the car door. I take her elbow and escort her up the steps. I hold the door open and then follow her inside.

"Welcome back." Gabriel grins at her before handing her a clipboard and a white wristband.

Kenzie turns and looks at me.

"It's a nondisclosure agreement. It's just a formality that applies to even my guests." I can't make an exception for her. I've impressed upon everyone who works here that rules are to be followed.

"Kenzie Stone, this grizzly bear is Gabriel Thorne. He's in charge of all things related to security for all our clubs."

"You have more than one adult's only club?"

"Two that are members only and two are nightclubs. Gabriel runs security for all four. He also deserves the credit for having the engine on your car repaired so quickly."

"You were in on it too?" Kenzie's face lights up with a smile as she extends her hand.

Gabriel accepts the handshake, and I swear he blushes. "Yes, ma'am. How's it running?"

"Like new, thank you." She lowers her head over the form. Thick lush hair falls over her shoulder, and she casually pushes it out of the way. She finally hands the form back to him. Judging by the amount of time it took her to sign, she read the entire thing word-for-word.

She slides on the wristband. "At least I didn't have to agree to turn over my firstborn son."

"No, ma'am. That's only if you join." Gabriel winks, walks to the inner doors, and opens them. "Any trouble, you ask for me."

"Do you have a lot of trouble here?" A frown creases her forehead.

"No, ma'am. None. Happy birthday."

"Thank you."

"That's right." I administer an imaginary head slap for forgetting. "I'm honored you chose to celebrate it with us." I take Kenzie's arm and lead her into the front area of the club.

"I didn't come to celebrate. I couldn't bring the money sooner because the invitation wasn't valid until today. There wasn't an address for me to mail the repayment, so I followed the directions on the back of the card."

"I'm flattered you kept the invitation."

She pauses and looks up at me. "I kept it as a constant reminder of what you did and that someday I would repay you."

My opinion of her jumps a few notches while at the same time my ego smarts. "Ouch. You haven't been suffering silently having to wait until today to see me?"

"Really? Be honest, did you remember me?"

"Damn right, I did." I offer her my arm. "My office is in the far corner, and the front section of the club is fairly safe for young eyes."

Her chin lifts and her brow furrows. "I'm not a puritan, nor do I judge people."

"Of course not, but you aren't part of this lifestyle." She's so incredibly beautiful with her bright eyes and lush lips that seem to be begging me to kiss them. A vision of her mouth wrapped around my cock while she takes it deep flashes through my mind. I picture her in restraints while I take my time enjoying her body.

If I had to guess, I'd say Kenzie has probably had only straight sex before, missionary style where the guy gets on top, drops his load, and then rolls off only to fall asleep. It's a damn shame too. A body like hers deserves to be worshiped.

I decide to launch into my sales pitch on the club. Talking will keep me from coaxing her to walk farther back into the scene area where she can see exactly how I live.

"This area is where people come to relax and have one of the club's free drinks. It's like any other bar where relaxing or talking is the main focus. The open scenes are on the other side of the dance floor and the rooms branch off from there. The social area and the dance floor are separated by a half wall. The disk jockey is an expert at keeping the mood light and sexy."

She pulls away and walks around the wall. I follow, stopping directly behind her. There are three pairs and one threesome on the dance floor. One woman has the top of her dress off her shoulders trapping her arms at her sides. She's sandwiched between two men who have her ample breasts in their hands while they dance. The others are more or less swaying to the beat. Kenzie turns and looks up at me.

"The trio moves as if they've done this before."

I stifle my surprise at her calm reaction. "They're polyamorous and regulars. I've never seen them when they weren't together." I put my hand on her back and guide her toward my office.

"This place used to be a hundred-year-old barn. We preserved what we could, using a great deal of the wood. The bar and workstations at each end are constructed out of lumber we couldn't use for posts and beams."

"What a great idea." She puts her hand on my bicep, and my dick perks up. "I love that you kept the history and ambiance alive."

"The far side, where we're headed, consists of tables, booths, and my office. You may see a Dom and his sub having a drink. Occasionally, it gets sexual, but they'll usually move to the scene area."

"In the books I've read, they were sectioned off but not private."

"It depends on the club; your author could be correct about other places. This section is open, but there are rooms farther back. It's up to the couple if they want privacy." I pay close attention to Kenzie's facial expressions, watching for her reactions. So far, other than her pupils being slightly dilated, she's not showing any outward signs of shock.

"The décor is beautiful and tasteful. You've done an excellent job. The black and gray with splashes of red create a festive atmosphere."

"Thank you. We put in many hours getting it ready."

Kayla Bianco spots us. She's out of the booth and is headed straight for us. Her husband, Nick Bianco, is one of the co-owners of our four clubs. His wife is bubbly, outgoing, and friendly. Maybe she can get Kenzie to relax. "It looks like you're going to meet a couple of my friends."

Kenzie pulls away. "I'm not planning on staying."

Before I can respond, Kayla is standing in front of us. She's wearing a barely-there camisole that laces up the front and tiny shorts that leave little to the imagination. She's smiling from ear to ear. "You didn't tell us you were expecting a date."

"No." Kenzie snaps out the word. "I'm not his date." She looks back and forth between us. If she's shocked at Kayla's clothes or lack thereof, she doesn't show it.

"Oh. I'm sorry," Kayla says. "If you're a single beginner, Slider will find the perfect Dom for you."

Fuck me. I figure that Kenzie is seconds away from running for the exit. She glances at me with wide eyes. No doubt, she sees I'm stumped on how to shut Kayla up because she lifts one shoulder and shrugs.

I jump in when Kayla takes a breath. "Kenzie Stone, this overzealous woman is Kayla Bianco. She's married to one of my partners, Nick."

"Pleased to meet you." Kenzie extends her hand. "I'm not looking for a Dom."

"I've never met a woman who originally thought she was, but when you find the right man, you'll know he's the one." Kayla loops her arm in Kenzie's. "Join us for a drink."

I bite back a laugh when Kenzie's mouth opens and closes, but she doesn't say a word. I'm not getting a judgmental vibe from her, and I like it. I follow along behind them, listening while Kayla chatters about her doubts and concerns about the lifestyle when she met Nick.

She stops as we reach Nick, who is standing and smiling at his wife. She introduces him to Kenzie before finally turning to me.

"Now, what were you trying to say before I stole this woman who isn't your date?" Kayla sits and pats the spot next to her.

"We're going to my office."

"Join us first. We only have a few minutes."

"Let me clear this up." Kenzie nods and then slides into the booth next to Kayla. "The only reason I'm here is to reimburse Justin for the repairs he had done on my car."

Kayla's eyes go blank for a second before she laughs. "You mean Slider?" She looks at me for a second. "I don't think I've ever heard your first name."

"Few have."

Nick clears his throat. "Regardless of the reason you came, it appears a misunderstanding has happened. Please stay. I'd like to hear about this noble deed my partner has done." He catches the attention of a passing server and orders a bottle of wine. "You must have made an impression on him because Slider isn't easily influenced toward niceties."

"Can you stop talking about me as if I'm not here? I stopped because she was broken down on the side of a busy highway."

"He did more than that," Kenzie continues. "Another man was there, insisting I go with him. Justin played along with me and made the guy think we were engaged." Kenzie drops the white envelope on the table in front of me. "I don't know what I would have done if he hadn't helped me out. The tow and repairs would've maxed out my credit card."

I lean back and listen as the story is repeated bringing back each detail. She's different in some way and when I hear her mention graduating college, I remember. She's found her dream job and is happy.

"Happy birthday," Kayla says. "Welcome to Satin."

The lights brighten and dim twice. Nick slides out of the booth and extends his hand to Kayla. "We should change." He turns to Kenzie. "I hope you'll stay for the demonstration. Kayla and I just returned from Greece where I studied Shibari under a renowned expert. We promised Slider our first exhibition would be here at Satin."

"Please do." Kayla leans into Nick as they walk down the hall, out of sight.

I push the envelope back in front of Kenzie. "Did any of those romance books you read touch on the art of Shibari?"

"Very few." Kenzie shifts in her seat.

She's uncomfortable, but it's hard to get a read on her. Is she interested or ready to bolt? "The demonstration is on the main stage in about ten minutes. Would you like to walk back to the seating area?"

Her breathing has picked up, but I'm not going to push it and risk losing her altogether. It happened to Nick and Kayla. It was almost a year later when he found out why she ran from Club Silken. It worked out for them, but I'm not going to push my luck. I'm curious about Kenzie's reason for coming here.

"Watching isn't required. How about I take you to dinner to celebrate your birthday?"

Her sparkling blue eyes meet mine, and blood floods my cock. "I am hungry. I didn't take time for lunch."

I stand and offer her my hand. "Me either."

We go to the lobby area, return the white bracelet she's wearing, and step outside into the night air. The temperature has dropped, and a light mist is falling. She shivers and runs her hands up and down her arms. I pull off my coat and wrap it around her shoulders. The breeze catches her hair, and it lifts in the air, sending the scent of flowers in my direction. I stifle the urge to bury my nose in her neck and breathe deeply.

"Thanks."

She makes no effort to walk forward. "I can sense you're changing your mind." I slip my finger under her chin and lift. My skin must be cold because she flinches, then catches my hand between hers and rubs. The shock that runs up my arm has me reconsidering the wisdom of me taking her anywhere.

"It's getting late, and I don't like leaving my car here."

"I'll make you a deal."

"What's that?"

"You drive. You can drop me off at my apartment after we've eaten."

Her eyes widen. My offer has surprised her. Fuck, it surprised me too.

"Well?"

"Deal. It's too cold to argue."

We walk to her car, and I hold the door while she shrugs off my coat and then slides behind the steering wheel. I lean in, reach across her, and buckle her seatbelt. Her sharp intake of breath pleases me. I step back, missing her face by inches. I close her door and then make my way to the passenger side, placing my coat in the back before settling into my seat.

"Did you think I was going to kiss you?"

"I didn't think anything." She reaches across me, opens the glove box, and pulls out a set of keys.

I start to question the wisdom of leaving her car open to theft, but she places the envelope holding the cash in my lap, interrupting my thought. I put it in the glove box.

"Liar. Did you want me to kiss you?"

"If I did, it's too late so why should I answer that question?"

My mind is going back and forth. This is a mistake. For her sake, it has to be. "You shouldn't."

She starts the car and drives onto the narrow road that leads from the club to the main highway. The distant city lights point the way.

"Tell me something about yourself," she says. "Other than your profession."

A low groan rumbles from my chest. I'm my least favorite subject. "There are better topics to cover."

"Oh, come on." She uses a teasing tone. "I'm sure there's more to you than meets the eye."

"You think so?"

"I know you are kind but not willing to admit it. You're obviously a good friend. Kayla and her husband seem to like you. You have a predilection for bossing women around." She taps her finger to her lips. "Oh, yes. You're not a serial killer." She glances at me, probably expecting to see at least a smile. Instead, I shake my head.

"You're a piss-poor judge of character."

"I'm no such thing."

"I think you are." She can't fathom the life I live. She has no idea the kind of man I am.

"So, enlighten me."

"I'm seldom kind. I'm selfish. However, I don't expect anyone to fawn over me because of it. I'm bossy and demanding, but I've never forced a woman to do anything she didn't want to do and will be damned if I ever do. If it becomes necessary to take such a drastic step, the relationship has gone to hell, and it's over. A responsible Dom ensures his sub knows what's expected. She does those things because it pleases her to please him."

She opens her mouth to speak, but I place my hand on her knee and squeeze. "And you do not know whether I'm a serial killer or not."

She reaches over and places her hand over mine. "I do know."

"Fuck." I pull away from her, lean my head back, and stare at the roof of her car. I want her. Want her spread across my bed cuffed to the headboard. She's in way over her head.

"If that's a suggestion, my response may not be what you expect."

I laugh but not because she's funny. It's because she's confirmed my suspicions. She's as naive as they come.

"I wasn't joking. What if I said yes?"

"I'm going to blame your curiosity on your love of research." If I don't end this right now, I'm going to hurt this girl. "Stop the car."

"What? Why?"

"Stop the fucking car."

She slams on the brakes, and both of us test the strength of her seatbelts. "There. Now what?"

"Why did you come to the club?"

"To pay you back."

"Then why didn't you leave it at the door with security?"

"I wanted to thank you."

"Is that the only reason?"

She doesn't answer me. Her head turns, and she stares into my eyes.

"I don't like to ask a sub twice. Answer me truthfully, or I'll pull you out of this car and spank your pretty ass until you do."

Chapter 2

Kenzie

I've been counting the days until I could see him again, and my hormones are running rampant. Yet, I'm struck dumb. Words are flying around in my mind at warp speed, but apparently, none are available for me to use. Why can't I just tell him I was drawn to him from the beginning? There's an internal prowess about him that exudes sex and sends flutters throughout my body.

The driver's door opens, and I shriek. "What are you doing?"

He leans in and unbuckles my seatbelt. "Get out."

I step outside in the night air and shiver. Anticipation that he might follow through on his threat to spank me has chills racing up and down my spine.

"I asked you a question." He steps closer, intimidating me with his size, and shielding me from the winter wind.

"Yes, I wanted to see you. After you dropped off my car, I hoped you'd get in touch, but you didn't. Now that I'm finally at a point in my life I can think about the opposite sex, I took advantage of your invitation. I didn't want to leave the money at the front desk."

"Go on."

"I've read a lot more about your lifestyle over the past seven months, trying to get a better idea of what goes with having a relationship with a Dominant."

"Then why didn't you want to watch the Shibari demonstration?"

"I would've if you'd said you wanted me to."

"Bullshit. I think you're too young to know what you want."

"I'm not a child." My blood boils through my veins. "A novice? Yes. The fact remains, I wanted to see you. To see if there was any mutual interest. So just tell me if there's not."

"If you're looking for a Daddy Dom, you've come to the wrong guy. If you have some romantic idea that we'll fall in love and live happily ever after, you've come to the wrong guy. If you're looking for someone who will let you play at being a sub, you've come to the wrong guy. I'm thirty-two years old, and I fuck hard and often. I control when I fuck, whom I fuck, and how I fuck. If you're looking for a less demanding Dom, I'll find you a partner to play with."

"I don't want anyone else."

His scowl does nothing to dampen my desire for him. He stares at me as if I've grown a second head. "Get in the car before you freeze."

"Yes, Sir." I put heavy emphasis on the *sir*.

"Fuck." He opens my door.

I don't hesitate to crawl inside and put the heater on maximum. Why can't I be attracted to one of the men at my new job? Because none of them send blood racing through my veins, yet every time I think of Justin, my body yearns for him.

He walks around to the passenger side, gets in, and studies me.

I squirm in my seat. "What now?"

"I want you to turn this car around and take me back to Satin. You need to spend some time thinking about what I said about my lifestyle, my way of living. You're an innocent."

"I'm not a virgin if that's what you're suggesting."

"I wasn't. You're seven years younger than me. Trust me, your experience is limited and when it comes to how I live, you are innocent. Be sure you know what you're asking for."

I make a U-turn on the gravel road and deliver him to the front door of the club. "And when I'm sure?"

"Come back or don't. I owe you a spanking. If you walk into my club again, I'll deliver." He opens the door and steps out into the cold. I watch as he leans in, grabs his coat from the back seat, and slips it over his broad shoulders.

"Justin," I call out before he closes the car door. He leans down to eye level and lifts an eyebrow.

"It's Slider. No one but my mother calls me Justin."

"Slider, do you want me to come back?"

His chest rises and falls as he breathes deeply. His gaze captures mine, and I see pure lust looking back at me. His blue eyes darken as he holds the stare for what seems like forever. That look alone has my lower region heating up. He knows I want him to say yes.

"I won't answer that until I know your decision."

****

I spent my Sunday prowling the internet for facts and reading blogs so I could add to what I'd learned about BDSM. Various toys used for spanking keeps coming up in my search. I wonder if I go to the club again, will he actually spank me, even if I say no? And why do my nipples get hard every time he pops into my mind?

Last week, my first week on the new job, I felt as if I were out of step with the rest of the world. It's still odd and I need to pay attention; I shake off outside thoughts and concentrate on finishing up my assignment. Monday, after filling out my paperwork, Mr. Thornton, one of the junior partners, called me into his office and assigned me research for a case he's handling. He stated in no uncertain terms he wants to settle this out of court and needed the information by Friday. I've put together a comprehensive file on the employer in question and am certain our client will collect lost wages and damages even if it does go to trial. I type a summary and send it with the data to Mr. Thornton's email. It feels good to hit *send*.

"Done," I say loud enough for my coworker in the next cubicle to hear.

I stand and stretch, rolling my shoulders and stretching my neck. Madison steps from her workspace into mine and applauds. Well, it's more of a golf clap, but I smile and take a bow.

"Thornton is well-liked by the partners. If you make him happy, they'll know it."

"I gave him more than what he needed to win the case." I open the desk drawer and take out my purse. "I'm ready for a hot soak in the tub."

"No." Her lips form the perfect pout. "It's Friday night, and we're going to celebrate your hard work."

I open my mouth to refuse but close it again. Maybe being among a crowd of people will keep Slider from consuming my thoughts. "One drink and I'm out of there."

Madison's face lights up with a big smile. "You'll enjoy it. Socializing with your peers isn't always a bad thing."

"So you tell me."

We ride the elevator down to ground level and start the three-block walk to the Corner Bar. It's not a cool name for a club, but it's accurate location-wise. It's cold, having reached thirty degrees around noon, but it's six o'clock, and the wind chill has dropped the temperature even lower. I pull my sweater tighter while the wind whips around my bare legs. I feel a tug on my belt and look back.

"If you'll fucking slow down, I'll walk with you."

"Sorry, I'm freezing."

"No. You have long legs, and I don't. I'm almost jogging to keep up."

I chuckle at her as I shorten my steps. "Cardio is good for you."

We step inside the club and spot the small corner table that three of the other paralegals in the company have snagged. The music is loud, and the place is packed. It's nice and warm inside. The club is cozy in the style of an old English pub. I've seen pictures of an Ayrshire cow but never as the face of a clock. Behind the packed bar are more tap handles for ale and lager than all the brand-name beer in the states. We borrow unused chairs from tables and drag them over to join our coworkers.

Thomas has the cubicle on the other side of Madison, and he scoots the other two men closer together so we can squeeze in and join them. I hang my purse on the back of my chair and sit.

He leans across Madison and grins at me. "We just about decided you were too good for us. I'm glad you proved us wrong."

The server spares him from the curt response on the tip of my tongue. "I'll have a small draft beer. Something light."

This is all very new to me, and I have trouble joining the conversation. Hanging out with friends isn't something I've done a lot of. I've worked and gone to school since aging out of foster care. I didn't have time to get too close to anyone. It was self-preservation, I suppose. I learned at an early age people always move on. It was normal and expected.

I finish my second beer, stand, and pull my purse strap onto my shoulder. Everybody at the table says goodbye except Madison. She shakes her head and motions me to follow her. It's too loud to argue, so I trail her to the restroom hallway and stop at the door.

"I'm tired. I'll see you Monday morning."

"Are you too tired to have a drink with me?" The voice rips right through me, making my stomach do flips and heat spread through my body. I whirl around and look into the same blue eyes that have haunted my nights for a week.

"He's been staring at you," Madison says. Her hand clamps down on my shoulder. "That's why I had you come with me, so I could warn you that he's been watching you."

"She's safe with me. After all, she already knows I'm not a serial killer. Don't you, Kenzie?"

Madison's grip loosens. "You know this guy?"

"I do." I turn and she's staring at Slider with a gaping mouth. "Madison Walker, meet Justin Locke."

She reaches around me and shakes his hand before he turns back to me. "That drink?"

"I'd love one." I turn to Madison, and she's nodding her head.

"Go," she whispers. "I'll see you Monday."

Slider places his hand on my back, guiding me toward the front door. "I know a much quieter place."

A billion ants are racing around in circles under my skin. Has he been following me? I step outside and stop under the streetlight.

"How did you know where to find me?"

He leads me to a limo idling at the curb, opens the door, and waves me inside. "It's too cold to talk out here."

I slide inside, sinking into the butter-soft leather seats. Slider takes the seat across from me.

"You almost ran into me coming out of your building. I had some business to take care of, so I had my driver track where you went."

"I'm sorry I didn't see you. Don't tell me you have an office in the building?"

"No. The interior decorator redoing my apartment has an office on the fourth floor. She had a presentation ready for me to see."

"So, fate brings us together again."

"I can't say I'm disappointed." His gaze roves over my face and then down my body. The question is there behind his eyes. I wait to see if he's going to ask if I've considered his lifestyle.

"Ty, take us for a drive." Slider closes the privacy window and opens a compartment housing various bottles of alcohol. "What were you drinking?"

"Beer. I don't care for the hard stuff."

"Let's see what's here." He moves things around and produces a Heineken. "Will this do?"

"Absolutely." I feel the limo moving as we head toward the unknown.

He splits the beer into two glasses and hands me one. "Cheers." He raises his glass and takes a sip. "Do you believe in fate?"

I swallow, giving myself a second to think about his question. "I'm not sure. If so, I did something years ago to piss it off. Do you?"

His lips lift in that panty-melting smile. "I do now."

"In a city this size, running into you is nothing short of a miracle, so maybe fate does exist."

He nods and leans back in his seat. I wait for him to bring up our conversation, but he doesn't. The heat in the limo feels good, and soon I'm ready to take off my sweater. Slider puts his glass in a cupholder and assists me.

His body is close, and the same scent that gave me rubbery knees at his club fills my senses. He folds my sweater and places it on the seat beside me.

"Thank you." I've never been drawn to a person like this, and I have to tell him the truth. "I spent Sunday looking up things on the internet. I couldn't get you off my mind, and I have to be honest. It scares me a little."

He leans toward me and cups my cheek in his hand. "I understand how it would."

A laugh bubbles up and I can't hold it back. "Really?"

His eyes narrow. "You'd be a fool if it didn't."

My heart flutters. "I'm not scared of you. I'm scared I'll lose myself."

I don't realize he's moving until his free hand fists my hair and his mouth crashes down on mine. The kiss surprises me, but I lean into him. The taste of his tongue as it slips across my lips is minty and delicious. He adjusts the angle of my head and slides deeper inside me. He explores, maps, and silently promises things I've never dreamed of, at least not until I met him. His lips caress mine in unhurried strokes turning my blood into a raging fire. I grasp his shoulders as my tongue meets each thrust of his.

He pulls inches back, and I whimper. "I want to fuck you, but I need to hear you want me to." His face hovers over mine, waiting for an answer.

"Yes. God, yes. I want you."

Slider moves back into his seat but takes me with him. His powerful arm lifts me as if I weigh nothing. Pausing long enough to push my skirt up, he places me so I'm straddling his legs. His free hand pushes a button.

"Take us to my apartment."

His hand brushes my hair back over my shoulders. Long fingers stroke my neck, around to the front of my blouse, and then deftly unbutton me. He pushes it away from my breasts. His touch is light as it trails down my chest to the top of my bra. My nipples pebble and push against the lace, begging for attention. I moan when his thumb slides under the fabric and strokes me.

I watch him, trying to convince myself I'm not dreaming, and this is really happening. His tanned skin against my pale flesh is electric, and I press my breast into his touch.

"I've thought about this all week. Waiting to hear from you has almost driven me crazy." A finger slides in next to his thumb, and he rolls my nipple between them, pinching until I moan. "The things I want to do to your body. I want to give you more pleasure than you've ever imagined existed." He pulls back and stares into my eyes. "Know this going in. I'm monogamous when in a relationship. Any breach and it's over."

"I like that. I need one promise."

"Name it."

"When we're over. You'll tell me. No dragging it out, no unreturned phone calls, and no avoiding me. I need honesty. Don't just suddenly shut me out and leave me wondering what the hell happened. I'm a big girl. I can take it."

"You have my word."

Leaning forward, I kiss his neck, nuzzle his raspy stubble and breathe in that scent of the ocean and fresh air that is so intoxicating. I move to his mouth and nip his bottom lip before pulling it into my mouth and sucking on it.

"Fuck," he whispers into the kiss while rolling his hips and placing his erection against my panties.

"We're here," the driver says through the speaker.

"Good." Slider moves away from me and I miss his touch.

I button up as fast as I can, pull my sweater over my shoulders, and give him a quick nod. "Ready."

The limo barely comes to a stop when Slider's out with his hand extended to me. I grab hold, and he tugs me out and against his chest. One arm wraps around me, holding me in place.

"Go home, Ty. I won't need you again tonight." Slider reaches to close the door but pauses. He strokes my cheek with his fingers. "You're sure this is what you want?"

I'm lost in his gaze. It's raw and passionate and hungry. For a split second, I know how a rabbit feels when looking into the wolf's eyes. Unable to look away, I nod.

"Words. Say it in words."

"Yes. I'm sure."

He takes my hand and we enter the building, cross the massive lobby, and walk into an empty elevator that seems to be waiting just for us. Slider removes a card from his wallet, scans it, and pushes a button that wasn't an option before. He's as calm as if we were out for a stroll, while my beating heart is about to crack a rib. My mind is racing. What if I can't live up to his expectations?

He lifts my hand to his mouth and kisses my palm. "That's quite a grip you have."

I release my death hold and turn to face him. "My nerves are showing."

His thumb and finger catch my chin and tilt my head back. "One by one I'm going to peel off each of your layers until I know every one of your wants and needs. I'll own all of them." His head lowers, and his lips brush back and forth across mine.

The ding of the elevator pulls our attention away from each other. My body silently protests the interruption. We step into a large white open-concept space that includes a kitchen, dining, and living area. The flooring, the cabinets, and the countertops are white with random sweeps of pale gray. A massive dark gray leather couch and two matching chairs sit on the right of a wall of glass. The décor is cold, stark, and startling at the same time. I spot an autographed Cubs baseball on the end table. It stands out against its sterile surroundings.

"You're a baseball fan."

"I am."

Slider reaches around me and closes the door. His mouth covers mine. Like a baby bird begging to be fed, I open for him, and his tongue thrusts inside. I lean into him, my body responding to his touch.

He possesses me. Dominates me.

I'm not afraid of the fire he ignites. I need it. Welcome it.

He pulls my skirt up to my waist and then slides his hands around to my ass.

"Wrap your legs around me."

I do as he says, hearing my shoes land on the floor. I lock my ankles around him and grip his shoulders and grind my pussy into him. My back is slammed against the door, my head bouncing off it. I'm wedged between his solid body and wood. His tongue searches the inside of my mouth, touching every surface, mapping me as if staking a claim. He releases his hold on my ass, and I drop my feet to the cold tile flooring.

"Go upstairs and undress. Do what you need to in the bathroom because you won't be getting a chance for a while. Kneel next to the bed with your hands clasped behind your back."

His gaze is hot and intense. His blue eyes are beautiful and hypnotizing.

"Now."

Chapter 3

Slider

Kenzie blinks a couple of times, letting my instructions soak in.

"Go." I point toward the stairs. "It's the room at the end of the hall." She turns and almost runs up the stairs. I watch her bare feet climb until she's out of sight.

I can't cut her any slack. She needs to see the real me. I won't go vanilla with her and then try to show her my true self later. For her sake, I can't. Perhaps it will cure her curiosity and she'll move on. Deep down inside, if I'm honest with myself, I'll admit I hope she doesn't cut and run.

My cock is so fucking hard it hurts and has been since she walked into the club last weekend. I couldn't wait to see if she came back to me. Wouldn't take that chance. I've never let a woman affect me like this. My self-control is as important to me as her submission will be. I slow my breathing, counting the number of breaths I take. In and out. In and out.

I walk to my glass wall and look out over the city. I'm the only one in the nightclub partnerships still living in an apartment. Zack and Morgan bought a house outside of town closer to Club Silken, our first members-only club. Nick and Kayla purchased their home a few miles from them. It's not something I've ever been interested in doing, but the fact they've nested gives me something to rib them about.

I turn and look behind me at the stark white room. The layout is perfect and is the reason I recently bought this place. The décor isn't my style, but that's an easy fix and why I'm having it redone. The two extra bedrooms will be put to good use. A large part of my job can be done remotely so one will serve as a home office. I have detailed requirements for the room closest to the master bedroom. My playroom won't have everything Silken or Satin has, but I look forward to having one in my home.

A glance at my watch tells me she's been in the present position for about fifteen minutes. I can't wait to see if she followed instructions. Regardless of how badly I want to race up the stairs to her, I don't. I leisurely take one step at a time, then walk down the hall, stopping in the open doorway.

My jaw comes unhinged, and my mouth falls open. She's naked, in the middle of my bed with her hand between her legs. If I weren't so pissed, I'd tell her how beautiful she is and that I think she's presented me with the sexiest sight I've ever seen.

"What the fuck do you think you're doing?" If I was expecting her to be embarrassed, she's not. She stretches her beautiful body like a cat and grins at me, but there's no smile behind her eyes. This was deliberate. She's testing me. I stalk to the side of my bed. "Answer me."

"I thought you forgot about me. For all I know, you left."

I growl loud enough that she quickly sits up. "Did you do any research at all? My sub doesn't touch herself unless I give permission. Her pussy belongs to me. I decide if and when she comes."

She folds her legs under her ass. Her luscious breasts beg for my attention. My hands burn to touch her, but I don't move an inch.

"I spent two days trying to learn everything I could about BDSM and the different kinds of Dom/sub relationships." Tears fill her eyes and coat her eyelashes. "Now I learn you already have a sub? Then why am I here?"

"What are you talking about?"

"You said 'my' sub."

"I do not currently have a sub and haven't for a long time, but we're not talking about me. If you spent two days familiarizing yourself with BDSM, you knew what would happen when I caught you with your hand buried in your pussy."

"Yes, Sir." Her strawberry blond hair falls over her shoulders, the ends brushing her nipples.

Fuck me. I should tell her to dress while I call a car to take her home. Instead, I turn around and sit on the edge of the bed.

"Yet you did it anyway." She straightens her shoulders. "You were testing me. Why?"

"Not testing. It hurt my feelings that you just left me up here waiting."

"Come here and stretch out across my lap facedown. I still owe you a spanking, so I'll add it to the one you're about to get."

She wipes her cheeks with the backs of her hands and then crawls across the bed. She lies over my legs, the tips of her fingers brushing the carpet and her toes touching the floor. Damn, I love those long legs. I take the soft round mounds in my hands and massage. She stiffens under my touch.

"Have you ever been spanked?"

"More times than you can count." Her tone is filled with anger. She takes a deep breath. "Go ahead. Get it over with."

Her words pull me to a dead stop. I rest my hand on her back and realize her body is tense enough to snap like a twig. "Tell me about the spankings?"

"Do you want names or just the number of times?"

My heart drops to my belly. This beautiful woman has been beaten and more than once. Spankings as a teaching tool or in play may be the last thing she needs. I put my hands on her shoulders. "Sit beside me."

She pushes up and then folds herself into position next to me. The tears are gone, replaced with a look of resolve in her eyes.

"I'll schedule an Uber while I dress. Then I'll get out of your hair."

I cup her cheek in my hand and rub my thumb over her soft bottom lip. When she leans into me, I know she wants to stay.

"You need to learn how to trust. I understand how that may be hard for you, but without it, there is no relationship. You have to remember that your Dom will never lie to you. Never hurt you unless it's something you request."

She nods her head.

"Do you want to leave?"

"Why didn't you spank me? I could've taken whatever you dished out." She pulls her legs from under her and stands.

"Sit down." I pat the bed with my hand. She immediately responds, perching on the edge of the mattress as if she's going to bolt any second.

I've never considered taking on a sub who I thought was unsure of her needs, but I want Kenzie to stay. "There are many ways I can teach a sub how to become compliant or to remind her who makes the final decisions. I give you my word that I will never spank you, not with my hand or any implement."

Relief washes over her face. I think she wants to stay too. The desire to hunt down the person or persons who hurt her sends bitter bile to the back of my throat.

"Really?"

"Not unless you specifically ask me to." I stand and face her. "There's a fine line between pain and pleasure. Along with many different ways to punish you."

"Can we begin again? Please, Sir."

I unbutton my shirt. "Come here and finish undressing me."

She scrambles off the bed, only slowing down when her hands reach my shirt, which she pushes off my shoulders. Her gaze is on my chest, and she strokes her hand downward, running her fingers over me as if she's counting each muscle. Her eyes lift and lock with mine just before her pink tongue peeks out and strokes across her lips. She leans down and licks my skin next to the trail of hair that disappears under my belt.

"Jesus. Your tongue is electric." I kick off my shoes and shed my socks but leave

my slacks for Kenzie to remove. She unzips me and pulls my pants and underwear down to my ankles. I kick them aside and watch as my dick throbs right in her face. She reaches for me, but I catch her hand in mine. "No. I haven't given you permission to touch my cock."

I lead her to the bathroom, lay out two towels, and turn the multiple spray heads on. She's so fucking beautiful standing there, waiting for me to tell her what to do. It takes every ounce of willpower I have not to lean her over the sink and bury myself to the hilt inside her. Instead, I take her hand in mine, step in first, and pull her under the spray in front of me.

Neither of us speaks as I reach over her head and get the bottle of body wash from the shelf. I pour some in my hand, then rub them both together until I work up a lather. I wrap my fingers around her neck, stroking her soft silky skin before moving to her shoulders, across her collarbone to circle her luscious breasts. I cover the soft mounds with suds.

I pull and twist her nipples. Her back bows, offering herself to me. When a small gasp escapes, I can't resist her open mouth. My lips crash down on hers. My tongue slides past her teeth, tasting her. Her soft mewl sends heat lashing through my veins, and I deepen the kiss. She's delicious, and I explore every inch inside her mouth. She's a drug, one that makes me drunk on lust. Either my cock or my brain is going to explode, and I'm not sure which is going first.

Her arms are at her sides, and I realize she's waiting for my permission.

"Touch me."

Without taking her gaze off me, she sinks to her knees. Her hand circles my erection and strokes me. Her pink tongue slides across her lips before she licks the precum off the head. She stops, her eyes widen, watching me, waiting for permission for more than just her hand. I want her for my submissive, but I can't make that decision for her.

"Put my cock in your mouth."

She makes a soft humming sound, and she slides me inside, lapping me with her tongue. This isn't what I had in mind when we got into the shower, but I'm sure as hell not stopping her. I place my hand on the back of her head and press myself deep inside her, easing up when I think she's going to gag. She doesn't, only sucks me deeper. That fire rushing through my veins changes course and floods my cock.

"So good," I tell her while she cradles my balls in her hand and pulls back to kiss the engorged tip. "Your lips around my cock are beautiful."

Her cheeks sink in as she works me farther into her throat. Pumping and sucking, she holds my ass with both hands, her nails digging into my flesh. With each thrust, I get closer to the back of her throat. "All of it. Take it."

She looks up at me and relaxes her jaw and swallows until my balls are against her chin. Every inch of my cock is in her beautiful mouth. I want to savor it, but I'm about to explode.

"Fuck."

Kenzie mumbles as her tongue finds the small slit in the head of my cock. She laps at me. I take both hands and wrap her hair around my palms. All I can think about is how hot and wet the inside of her mouth is, and my willpower, which I'm normally proud of, slips away from me. I hold her head still and fuck her, pushing deep and pulling back and repeating the process until my balls tighten and streams of cum jettison from me.

I moan, the sound rolling off the tiles in the shower. "Fuck, yes." Her throat opens and closes as she swallows and swallows until I'm wondering just how much cum I gave her. She finally lowers her eyes as she slides my softening cock out and licks me clean.

I bend, grasp her arms, pull her to her feet, and kiss the hell out of her, all in one motion. She leans against me, her hands digging into my wet hair. We stay like this for a few minutes. Me kissing her lips, eyes, ear lobes, and her soft neck. I step back and smile at her.

"You are fantastic. I don't want to know who taught you to do that, because I might have to find him, thank him, and then kill him."

Her eyes flash wide, and her cheeks turn a shade of pink. Her expression is priceless, and I remember how young she is.

"I'm pleased you liked it. I wanted to taste you. Was I out of line?"

"No. I gave you permission." I reach behind her and pull a washcloth from the hook. "Let's finish our shower. I have to decide what your punishment will be."

Her eyes sparkle as she grabs the body wash and hands it to me. "Yes, Sir."

I finish washing her, taking delight in her moans and groans while I explore the inside of her pussy. She gasps, lifting on her toes when my finger circles her tiny rosebud. I put one hand on her shoulder, hold her still, and sink to the first knuckle in her tight hole.

"Don't fight me. I will have all your orifices. They belong to me." I slide in and out of her, watching as she closes her eyes. "I need words. Tell me."

"Everything I am belongs to you."

That's a heavy statement, considering she doesn't know all the dark things I want to do to her, but for now, her writhing on my finger is all I need to know. I remove it, rinse her off, open the glass door, and reach for a towel. "Step out and dry off. When you're done, kneel by the bed. Arms behind your back clasped at the wrists, your bottom sitting on your heels, and your gaze downward. You will remain so until I tell you otherwise. Do you understand?"

"I won't disappoint you."

I step between her and the door, cup her cheek in my hand, and wait until she realizes her mistake.

"Sir," she says quickly. "I won't disappoint you, Sir."

"Good catch." She's sharp and quick, a trait I appreciate. I take her lips hard, and my tongue assaults the inside of her mouth. Her hands come up and clutch my shoulders. I force myself to break away. "Go."

I finish my shower, dry off, and stand in the doorway with the towel around my waist. She's in the correct position. I hang up my towel and walk to her, circling but not speaking. I pause behind her, bend down, and run my hand between her legs. Her pussy is soaked, and my cock jumps from semi-hard to painfully rigid. I smile down at her satiny, naked skin. "Lie on the bed, hands above your head, legs spread."

I watch, doing my best not to pounce on top of her and fuck her blind. It would be the biggest mistake of my life if I don't try to make this happen between us. Kenzie will be the perfect sub if I don't push her too hard.

"Like this?" Her voice is soft, and I can barely hear her. She's nervous, and I like it.

I nod, walk to the head of the bed, pull the restraints from the bedside table, and hold them up for her to see. "They're made of a soft ribbon and won't hurt unless you fight them. Do not attempt to free your hands. If you get frightened, use your safe word. You need to choose one now."

"Red to stop, yellow means slow down, and green says go."

"You're correct. Those are the standard words. But you can select anything you want. Something you'll remember without having to think about it. If it's red, fine. Just be sure."

The tip of her tongue slips out of her mouth and slides across her lips. "Green, Sir. I'm very green."

I secure her hands, dropping a kiss on the inside of each wrist. As I lean over her, my fingers run down the underside of her arms to her luscious breasts. I cup them in my hands and tweak her tawny nipples to even harder peaks. Her back bows as she offers herself, and I accept by taking one of the tips into my mouth. Her moan has my cock pulsing. I glance up to find her watching me. I gently tug her rigid peak with my teeth, and a soft cry escapes her lips.

"You are so fucking perfect."

"Please," she whispers.

"Please? You want to come?"

"Yes, please." Her hips squirm from side to side.

I move to the other breast, repeating the same process on this nipple. The mewling sounds coming from Kenzie are driving my cock to the point of pain. I cup her mound and then slide one finger inside her folds. I pull some of her juices to her clit with my thumb. She bucks into my hand, and I pull away.

"No. Don't stop. I was so close."

I smile down at her, enjoying the frustration in her expression. "Denial of an orgasm can be as much of a punishment as spanking. That was your first denial, and you owe me another."

Her eyes flash fire for a second, and she opens her mouth as if to say something, but she hesitates.

"Go ahead and say it. I need you to tell me what you think, what you feel, and what you want."

"I want to come."

"I know you do." This time I slide down her body and open her folds with my thumbs and study her swollen pussy. She squirms under my scrutiny. "You are beautiful. Pink and wet and swollen."

"Please." Her eyes follow my every move.

I like that she wants to see everything. My hands slide under her hips, and I lift her so she can watch when I flatten my tongue and lick from back to front before sinking inside her vagina. I drink from her as if I'm starving until I feel the first shudder. Reluctantly, I pull myself away.

"No." She struggles against the restraints but stops. "Please, spank me. Do what you want, but let me come."

Her clit is hard and swollen, so I lightly slap it with my fingers. "Maybe I'll spank your pussy."

"Yes." She lifts her hips higher offering herself to me. "Please, do that again."

I tap her clit again, not too hard but enough that she feels it.

Her mouth drops open and her eyes close. "More, please."

I can't make her wait any longer. I grab a condom from the bedside table and cover myself. Once I'm in position, I glide my cock back and forth in her juices, getting myself slick before sliding the engorged head into her. I drape her legs over my shoulders and slam home. I fill her, bottom out at her cervix, and stop, pausing to let us both feel the complete connection. Her eyes slowly open and she smiles. *Fuck me.* She makes me feel like a king.

"Slider. You're huge. I feel so full."

"Not too big to be the perfect fit for you." I don't correct her for using my name instead of sir. There's time for that later. Right now, all I can think of is the heat surrounding my cock as I pull out and slide back deep. Her pussy grips me, tugging me still deeper. I start a rhythm that increases with each thrust. The soft sounds of pleasure she makes fill the air around me. I put all my weight on one arm and roll her nipple between my thumb and finger. I pride myself on stamina, but I'm hanging on to the edge with everything I have.

Her gaze locks with mine, and I see the question in her eyes.

"Come." I press her clit with my thumb.

Her mouth opens and words come out, but they're jumbled together and are just sounds. The first wave of her orgasm hits her, and she tightens around me. Her body bucks while she spasms around me. I hold back. I'm not about to come yet.

"God. Oh. My. God."

I reach up and untie her hands, and she grabs my shoulders, sinking her nails into my flesh. Her hips meet every thrust I give until she drops her head back against the pillow.

"Again." I pull out and roll her over on her hands and knees.

"I can't."

"You can and will." I slam back into her wet heat. I lean over her body and massage her breast before moving to her already sensitive clit. She is so responsive it only takes a couple of pinches, and she's rocking back onto my cock, and a slow moan rolls from her as she shudders through a second orgasm.

I increase my pace and relish the sensation as her tremors clutch me, dragging me deeper until I can't hold on any longer. Waves of cum jettison from me, again and again, filling the condom. At last, I pull us onto our sides. I quickly dispose of the condom and roll back, pulling her into my arms.

She's very still and quiet so I push her long hair off her face and kiss the top of her head. I break into a smile no one but me can see. Kenzie is sound asleep. I turn out the light and join her.

Chapter 4

Kenzie

I cuddle against the warm body snug against mine. It only takes me a second to remember whose arm is draped across my stomach and erection is pressed against my butt cheeks. His warm breath stirs my hair. I stay very still, keep my eyes closed, and enjoy the Egyptian bed sheets under and over me. I want to enjoy the afterglow of a Friday night well spent for as long as I can.

"Good morning." Slider's hand skims over my skin, sending chill bumps to my breast, where he cups me in his hand.

"I guess this means I don't have to leave right away."

"Yes, it does."

I snuggle against him, and he tugs at my nipple. A slow throb between my legs has me hoping we're going to have morning sex.

My eyes fly open. A massive wave of humiliation washes over me. I grab the soft sheet that's covering us and pull it over my face. "I'm sorry." I rethink my words and quickly add, "Sir."

Slider chuckles and tugs the soft sheet down until my eyes are exposed. "What exactly do you need to apologize for." The corners of his mouth lift into a smile and his eyes twinkle like stars.

"I can't believe I fell asleep."

"I took it as a compliment."

"That's right." I nod my head like a bobblehead doll. "I was complimenting you."

"You went down hard. I figured the warm washcloth I used to clean you last night would wake you, but it didn't."

"Oh, God." My cheeks are burning so I bury my face into the pillow. "Don't tell me anything else."

He turns my head slightly, leans over me, and strokes his lips across mine, soft yet firm. His tongue slides inside my mouth. He tastes minty and tempting.

"You taste good," I whisper against his lips.

"That's because I've had my shower and brushed my teeth." He rolls me over on my back and then wedges his body between my legs.

Panic bubbles up inside me. I hate to bring it up, but I have to go. "I really should go to the bathroom."

Slider lifts up, chuckles, and places an open-mouth kiss at the top of my mound. "Go. I'll start breakfast."

"But…"

"Maybe I'll have you for dessert."

He moves off me and I scramble out of bed. My trip through the bathroom includes a shower and the use of a new unopened toothbrush I find next to the sink. I borrow the brush on the counter, put my hair in a long braid, and venture into the bedroom to where my clothes are on the floor. After wearing them all day yesterday and tossing them aside last night, they look pathetic, so I head to his closet for a robe.

In all the romance books I've read, and that's a lot, the heroine sometimes wears the hero's shirt, but I'm looking for something different. My search doesn't yield a robe or anything close to one, but I spot a Bears jersey and quickly pull it on. Even though I'm tall, he's taller, and the tail of the shirt hangs a couple of inches below my bottom.

"Five minutes," Slider calls out.

"Coming." I jog down the stairs, following the aroma of bacon. I stop and watch for a second. He's barefoot, wearing only a pair of warm-up pants that hang loosely on his hips. His body is perfect, and any sculptor would love to have Slider as a model. His broad shoulders and muscular arms frame his torso perfectly.

"Are you finished looking?"

"Almost." I wish he'd turn around, but he doesn't.

"Then grab the plate, napkin, and silverware on the bar and set the table." Holding a frying pan in his hand, he turns and nods at the breakfast bar.

I cross the living room to the counter but stop and study the items. What the hell does this mean? "There's only one place setting."

"That's correct. Put it at the head of the table."

"Yes, Sir." I don't hesitate to do as instructed but can't help but wonder which one of us gets to eat. I return to the kitchen where he's scooping a large helping of scrambled eggs onto a platter next to a pile of bacon.

"Is that the best you could find to wear?"

"Is this like a sacred shirt or something? I can go change."

"Not it all. It hides too much of your body. Grab that carafe of coffee."

I pick up the pot and follow him like a puppy dog, waiting to see who gets fed and who doesn't.

He puts the platter down, and I set the coffee next to it. Then Slider pulls a chair back, sits, and pats his lap. "Come here."

"Really? I've read this in books but didn't know it was true." Eyes wide, I sit in his lap. The aroma of food fills my senses, and my stomach rudely growls. "Excuse me. I don't know if it's the food or you, but suddenly I'm starving."

"Good." He reaches around me and fixes his plate as if I'm not in the way. His lips graze my cheek while he works. "Cream and sugar?"

"Just cream, please." I'm happy there are two cups on the table. He spreads a napkin across my lap, then fills a fork with eggs and presents it to me. I greedily take it into my mouth and slide the food off with my lips. The flavor bursts in my mouth and melts on my tongue. I moan my approval.

"Taste good?" He breaks a slice of bacon into two pieces, puts half in his mouth, and gives the rest to me.

"Hmm." I nod and shift my weight in his lap.

"Be still." He moves me closer to his knees. "You wiggle, I get hard, then breakfast gets cold."

"Oh. Sorry." I can't help but smile. I like that I have that much control over him.

We eat in silence, and within minutes, the food is gone. He pushes an empty chair away from the table with his foot. "Sit over there."

It's so sudden I wonder if I've done something wrong. I have to stop worrying about upsetting people as I've done in the past. I'm self-supporting now and can speak my mind. I do as he said, pulling the Bears shirt down to cover at least some of my bare leg. I slide my coffee in front of me and take a long sip. I set the cup in its saucer and wait for him to start the conversation.

Slider watches me silently. His lips have a slight lift at the edges but it's not a smile. He leans forward and catches my wrist, which he inspects. "I didn't hurt you last night, did I?"

"Not at all."

"Tell me about your spankings."

"Really?"

"If I tell you to do something, there's no reason to question it."

"That's a Dom thing?"

"Who spanked, no, beat, you?"

My hands automatically clench, and my nails dig into my palms while my chest feels as if a leather band is wrapping around me, getting tighter by the second. I knew our conversation would eventually turn personal, but my childhood isn't something I like to talk about. "Are you going to be as honest with me as you expect me to be with you?"

"I'll never lie to you. You may not like what you hear, but it will always be the truth."

"I can live with that."

"Tell me."

"Long story short, I lived in six different foster homes from the age of six to when I aged out at eighteen. A couple of them were great but overcrowded. The others weren't the best place for a girl."

The nerve in his jaw twitches. "You were abused?"

"No." I stare into his eyes. "Almost. I learned to defend myself."

"I'm sorry you went through that."

"That's all behind me, and I try to remember the places where I felt safe."

"Safe"—Slider leans forward in his chair—"not loved."

I feel my lip curl. "It's hard to feel loved when you never know how long you're going to be there. Anything was better than living with my mom, but I didn't understand that at the time. It's not my favorite topic of conversation."

He nods and stands. Let's get the kitchen squared away. I need to run a few errands."

I try to decide if that's a subtle hint for me to leave. "My cell is in my purse. Let me find it and I'll arrange an Uber to pick me up."

"What? No. Go with me. We can swing by your place so you can change."

"Sounds good to me." I grab the few dishes on the table and carry them to the kitchen. I can't figure him out, but I'm drawn to him and have been since I kissed his cheek on the side of the road seven months ago.

We start the dishwasher and head upstairs. On the top step, his hands slide under my shirt and cup my ass cheeks.

"Time for dessert," he whispers in my ear.

I walk to the bed, pull off the jersey, and drop into position.

His groan sends heat rushing through me. "You're going to be the death of me."

***

I unlock my door and walk inside my apartment. It's a lot smaller than Slider's, and the furniture isn't expensive, but I love it. "Welcome to my home."

He follows me inside. His gaze scans the living, dining, and kitchen area in one sweep. "I like it. You have good taste."

"Thanks." I'm flattered and pleased he doesn't comment about its size and my bargain-store decorations. "Everything you see is mine. Bought and paid for by me. Now that I have everything I need here, I've started saving for a newer model car." My eyes flash wide. I've been so deep into Slider, I've forgotten everything. "My car. I left it in the parking lot at work."

"I'm sure it will be fine."

"I can't believe I forgot something so important." I shake my head. "What if it's been towed?"

"I doubt that happened but if it did, I'll take care of it."

"I'd prefer to go get it and drive it home."

"We can do that. Do you want to change clothes first?"

"Yes. It won't take a second." I race to my bedroom, slip on clean underwear, jeans, a shirt, and a pair of comfy tennis shoes. "I'm ready."

Slider turns away from the window and his mouth drops open. "Fuck me."

I come to a stop in front of him. "What?"

"You look so young."

"Well, I'm not. I think I proved that to you last night and this morning. Don't try to use the age card to get rid of me, because it won't work."

His eyes sweep my body, sending chills across my skin. "I don't want to be rid of you."

"I also have a mind of my own and an independent streak that might be worth you rethinking a relationship with me."

His head falls back, and a laugh rolls from his chest. The sound fills the room, and I want to hear it again.

"When you're not with me, your 'independent streak' as you call it will probably serve you well. When we're together, it could get you disciplined. Note I didn't say would, I said could."

He stands, pulls a card from his wallet, and offers it to me.

"I understand."

"Let's go get your car. Think about what you truly want. If it's me, call this number. My driver will pick you up and bring you to the club tonight. If I don't see you, I'll accept it as a no."

"Fair enough." My mind is racing around like a dog chasing its tail. I like that he's not pressuring me, yet at the same time, I want him to encourage me to come.

He's a little distant as we leave my apartment and drive downtown to the parking garage where my car is parked. Slider stops and gets out of his sports car and walks around to help me get out. My emotions are all over the place. I want to throw myself into his arms. I want to know if he's sincere. I want to know if he wants me to call.

His thumb hooks under my chin, and I raise my eyes to meet his. His hands span my waist, his lips meet mine, and his tongue slides across, then inside. It's not a dominating, blood-and-guts kiss. It's seductive, sensual, firm yet soft, subtle, and provocative as he licks the crease, prompting me to open. My hands circle the back of his neck, and I moan.

He lifts his head and I almost cry out. "You are fucking perfect."

"So are you."

"If you show up tonight, Monday we'll get blood tests. My doctor will send the order to a lab near your work."

"I'm on the pill, so I like that idea."

"He'll expedite the results."

I dig out my keys and get into my car. I like that he waited until I start the engine and drive away. A strange feeling settles in my chest. I've felt it before but somehow it's different. *Will I lose myself to his dominance? Or find my true self?*

I drive straight to the nearest Victoria's Secret. Thirty minutes later I'm carrying a bag out of the mall with a matching champagne bra, thong, and thigh-high stockings. On my way out, a window display catches my eye. I walk inside and try on the super-short black skirt with a low-neck silk blouse of the same color. I change back into my clothes, pay the clerk, and drive home, feeling pretty damn proud of myself. There's nothing to think about. My decision is final.

I catch myself smiling as I climb the stairs to my apartment. I go inside, hang up my new clothes, and pull the card Slider gave me from my pocket. It takes another thirty minutes to work up the nerve, but finally, I call his driver.

"This is Ty."

"Hi. My name's Kenzie. Slider gave me this number."

"Yes, ma'am. I'm to pick you up and take you to him. When will you need me?"

"I'm thinking eight tonight."

"I'll be outside your apartment building when you come out."

"You have my address?"

"Yes, ma'am."

"Can you keep this between just you and me?"

"Excuse me?"

"I want to surprise him."

"That's not a good idea."

"Please?" He's quiet for a minute, so I check my phone to see if he's disconnected the call.

"If he needs me or asks where I am, I won't lie to him. That's the best I can do."

"Thank you."

I walk to my bed, stretch out, and stare at the ceiling. Slider thinks I'm too young. Well, this kid has lived through more in her twenty-five years than a lot of people. I take my cell out, set an alarm, and wrap myself around a pillow. I want to learn everything he can teach me, and I'm not afraid to ask for it.

Chapter 5

Slider

I push away from my desk, stand, and look at the time. *Fuck*. It's only been ten minutes since I last checked. I walk out into the open scene area. Satin is full tonight, but weekends have been that way since we opened. Danielle probably has her hands full on the floor. One of our monitors is out sick, and I don't like leaving one inch of the club unprotected.

I stand to the side and observe a Domme discipline her sub. Dressed in black leggings, heels, and a corset, she moves around him, completely in charge while she leaves red stripes on his body. She pauses and rubs the marks with her hand before leaning down and kissing each one. Just as I think she's through, she slaps the leather tip of the riding crop across the fleshy part of his ass. His body is covered in sweat, and he cries out in pain. She puts away the crop, lays a blanket over him, and whispers something I can't hear. He rises and follows her toward the aftercare area.

I turn toward my office, but one of the monitors stops me.

"There's a woman at the bar asking for you."

"Thanks." My heart rate picks up a notch as I stride to the front of the club, stopping just shy of the bar. I scan the area but don't see Kenzie.

"Looking for me, I hope?"

My stomach clenches as I turn to face her. "Rachel, how did you get in?"

Rachel reaches inside the spandex top she's wearing and pulls out a black membership card. "My husband's card."

"It should have been deactivated the day you were banned from the club. That's our mistake." I reach for it, but she shoves it inside her top. I'm not going after it.

She presses her body against mine. "I know you kept it active so I'd come scene with you."

"You're delusional." How the fuck she got past Gabriel in the foyer is a question I need to be answered. "You're violating the restraining order. Leave or I'm calling the cops." I take out my cell and text Gabriel.

"I'm divorced now. We can play whenever we want."

My blood pressure spikes just remembering the rumors she spread about me being in love with her. "It's never going to happen."

"Why are you acting so mean?" she whines.

Over her shoulder I see Kenzie staring at us. I peel Rachel off me and walk toward Kenzie, who has turned her back to me and is leaving. "Fuck."

Gabriel steps inside the club and slows her down. "Leaving so soon?"

"No." I wrap an arm around her shoulder. "She's not going anywhere."

Eyes cold as an iceberg meet mine. "I shouldn't have surprised you. It was a mistake."

"It wasn't a mistake. It's a wonderful surprise." Anger boils through my gut. I turn to Gabriel. "How did that nut case get in here?"

His frown tells me he doesn't know what I'm talking about. "Who?" He looks behind me. "I have no idea. I must've been in my office putting Ms. Stone's paperwork away."

I'm fucking thrilled she made her way to the club on her own, and I'm dying to read her interests and limits, but that will have to wait.

"Rachel has her husband's black membership card. Get it back and make sure it's deactivated this time." I glance over my shoulder and see Rachel coming toward us. "If she doesn't give it to you, call the cops. She's not leaving with it."

"No problem." Gabriel motions at a couple of monitors and heads for the bar.

"Will you come with me to my office?"

Kenzie's gaze hasn't left my face. A mixture of confusion and anger fills her eyes. "You don't have to explain your actions to me."

"My actions?" I say a little too loudly.

"Is she one of your lovers or trainees?"

"Neither. You're my only lover, and I haven't trained in years." I push down my anger at her immediate belief that I've lied to her. "I'm also not standing in the middle of the club explaining myself to you."

Kenzie glances around us as if she forgot where she is. Her mouth opens and closes. "I'll go."

I wrap my arm around her waist. "Not a chance. At least not until we talk." Before we can get to my office, I have to deal with Rachel. She and Gabriel are in our path. I catch Kenzie's chin with my fingers and turn her head to look at me. "Remember we talked about trust. Now's the time to demonstrate some."

We block Gabriel's path bringing them to a halt. Rachel opens her mouth, but I ignore her. My attention is on Gabriel. "Did you get the card?"

"No. And short of violating her by digging around in her bra, I think it's time to call the cops."

"Who gave you the card?" I again ask Rachel.

"Don't lie in front of your new sub." She's not looking at me. Her eyes are cold, crazy, and pinned on Kenzie. "You did."

"Gabriel, escort Rachel in your office and call the police." Kenzie stiffens under my hand. "I'll explain later."

Kenzie steps closer to Rachel. "You don't want to spend the night in jail, do you?" Kenzie extends her hand. "Give me the card, and I'll make sure you aren't arrested."

Rachel's lips curl into a snarl. "Fuck you."

"Sorry. You're not my type." My girl smiles, shrugs her shoulders, and moves back next to me. "Her choice."

"Fine." Rachel reaches into her blouse and retrieves the black card, handing it to Gabriel. Her eyes are cold as she glares at Kenzie. "Don't get used to being his sub. He'll come for me."

Kenzie and I walk to my office. By the time we get there, I have a raging hard-on. As soon as I get her inside, I lock the door behind us.

"That was—"

My hands go to her hips. I jerk her against me and cut off her words with my mouth. I devour her. Pressing hard and sliding my tongue between her lips, I taste every inch of her sweetness. Her hands come up and into my hair, pulling at the strands and holding me tightly. I want her. Want inside her. Want to dominate every inch of her. But we need to set the record straight. I reluctantly break contact with her glorious mouth. "Come sit next to me. You have questions about Rachel, and I have the answers."

Kenzie beats me to the couch.

"Ask away."

"It's none of my business. It's not like we're in a relationship. We're just exploring."

"Bullshit. We're back to that word trust again. I regret promising not to spank you. I told you the truth. I don't train subs and haven't had one of my own in years. You are the first woman I've wanted for more than one night in a long time. What part of that don't you remember?"

She blinks a couple of times. "This"—she waves her hand back and forth between us—"happened so fast, and I'm not used to having anyone taking care of me."

I sit beside her, turning her to face me. "Rachel and her husband were members of Silken for a while. He was never a devout Dom but came because it made her happy. They asked Zack to set up a third partner for a scene and I happened to be there."

"She's beautiful. You were lovers?" Kenzie tries not to stiffen, but I see her shoulders tighten.

"Not lovers. Partners. Once. Rachel started asking for me every time they came to the club. Complaining to Zack, one of the co-owners, when I refused. We both explained to her several times that my one-time participation was simply a courtesy of the club."

"A courtesy? Does that happen often?"

"A lot of members who come to play are not interested in finding a lover. They want sex with no emotional ties. But Rachel turned that one instance around and tried to make it into something bigger, more significant.

"They stopped coming for a while, but then she started showing up alone. Waiting in the parking lot for me, issuing demands, and refusing to listen to reason. It didn't take long until Zack revoked their membership. That's when she started coming to Gallant, the club I was responsible for in the city."

"There's another club like this?"

"Yes, Silken was the first member's only club we opened. But Gloss and Gallant are straight-up nightclubs." I lean over and brush my thumb across Kenzie's bottom lip. I need to touch her, and she must know it because her tongue slips out and caresses me. "Rachel's verbal attacks at Gallant resulted in a loss of customers. Her attacks turned into tires being slashed and car windows being broken. The security tapes proved who was responsible. A judge fined her and issued a restraining order."

"Wow. I'm guessing women stalkers are just as bad as men. I'm sorry for both of you."

"Both?"

"She's hurting. Feeling rejected and unworthy. I can sympathize with that."

"You're a much better person than me." Kenzie's right. This, whatever it is between us, has happened fast, and I know little about her. "Are we done with that subject?"

"Yes, Sir."

"If you ever see me in a situation you don't understand, I expect you to give me the benefit of the doubt. You assumed the worst tonight, and suspicious minds don't form lasting relationships."

She tilts her head, and a soft smile pulls at her lips. "Are you going to punish me for doubting you?"

"Maybe later." I stand, take her hand, and help her up. "Let's take a turn through the club. You may see something you'd like to try."

"I can't wait."

We walk out into the quiet area where people can sit, chat, and have one of the two drinks allowed. "You look stunning tonight. I'm glad you decided to come."

"It was supposed to be a surprise."

"It was quite a surprise. How you got Gabriel to join in is a mystery."

"He didn't know about it until I showed up in the parking lot." She looks up at me. Her eyes sparkle with mischief. "He likes me."

"Obviously, or he would've alerted me you were here." I lead her past the dance floor, take a left at the first aisle, and walk past the divider to an area where we can watch.

"Seeing it live is a lot different than reading it in a book."

"Yeah. It's a lot more fun this way." I snug her against me and let her take her time watching two men pleasuring each other. One rolls the other guy onto all fours and then coats himself with a bottle of lube sitting next to the bed. His partner watches over his shoulder as the rigid cock is rubbed in circles around his ass hole before sliding inside.

Kenzie appears to be mesmerized. She stares as he thrusts back and forth, and the sounds of passion come from them both. The man on top says, "I love you," to his partner, and she turns to face me.

"They're a couple?"

"We have quite a few members who are married or in a committed relationship."

"Like your friends Nick and Kayla?"

"Yes. Committed couples, like Nick and Kayla, wear a purple bracelet. Everyone in the building knows not to ask if they can join in a scene. Some of our members are single. They come in looking for a partner for the night. They don't want to form a connection." I take Kenzie's hand in mine. "Let's move on."

A loud snap fills the air, followed by a cry that startles her. "That sounded like it hurt."

I don't answer. This is something she needs to see for herself. We bypass a couple of scenes, stopping when we reach the couple in the last open area. "This is Bonnie and Earl," I say in a soft voice. "She left word at the bar that she was available for a punishment scene but with no sex."

"Really? What's the point?"

"She's a top executive for a worldwide company and under a great deal of stress every day. Occasionally, she stops by and turns over control to someone else."

"Wow."

I start to move on, but Kenzie's feet seem rooted to the spot. I move behind her, place a hand on each hip, and allow her to devote her attention to the couple. Bonnie is naked, on her knees, and bent over a padded spanking bench. Her chest rests on the top and her arms are extended forward where her hands are secured at the wrist. Earl is whispering in Bonnie's ear. One hand holds a leather crop. There are bright pink welts on her ass cheeks. He nods, walks to the rack, and places the riding crop in the used tray. He selects a wooden paddle from the hanger on the wall and smacks it across his hand.

Kenzie leans her head back against me. I like how her height puts her tucked under my chin. My cock is at half-mast, but I'm not about to move.

"Oh, God." A full-body shiver races over her body.

I move her hair to one side and kiss her neck, slowly moving to her jaw. "Earl is one of the best. He'll do exactly as she asks."

Earl stands behind Bonnie and again massages her ass. "Count them. I'll stop at ten."

"Yes, Sir."

The first blow draws a low moan from the sub. Each strike lands in a different spot, each blow harder than the last. I move us a couple of steps to the side so Bonnie's face can be seen. When she cries out the number eight, Kenzie's body goes rigid against me.

I don't want her panicking. "Let's move on."

"No. Please. Let me stay."

I'll yield my authority in this instant to Kenzie. She feels compelled to see the punishment to the end, and I won't refuse her.

Nine and ten slaps of the paddle finally land on Bonnie's bright red ass. Earl drops the paddle on the floor, quickly walks to the front of the bench, and releases her hands. He pulls a wipe from a nearby container and holds his face inches from hers as he wipes her brow and cheeks. Their conversation is quiet and short. He helps her to stand before sweeping her into his arms. Without making eye contact with anyone, they disappear around the corner.

"He's taking her to the aftercare area where he'll wrap her in a warm blanket, give her water and a couple of pieces of chocolate. They usually talk for a while before she dresses and leaves."

"She cried out but never shed a tear. It had to hurt like hell."

"But she's leaving with a huge smile on her face. To one person it's pain. To another it's pleasure."

Kenzie slides her hand in mine. "What's next?"

My cock springs to full alert. It's taken a colossal effort not to maul her while she watched the spanking. "I have a private room for us."

"I can't wait."

Chapter 6

I step inside the room and look around. The bed is the largest I've ever seen. The deep red spread holds at least a dozen pillows of every size and shape. A white chair with a plaid blanket over the arm sits next to a small table, which is beside a mirror on a stand. One wall is all racks and cabinets. Whips and paddles of every size hang from a shelf next to canes and ropes of assorted sizes and colors. The countertop has a glass bin with different vibrators, plugs, small pieces of metal, which I'm sure are nipple clamps. There are towels, tissues, bottles full of lube, and wipes. Lots of wipes. I see at least four boxes.

His eyes follow me as I move around the room. I know there are certain behaviors expected of a sub, so I stop, stand still, and wait for instructions.

"Once I close this door, you follow my rules. You respond to me as Sir. You don't nod if I ask a question; you answer me with words. As your Dom, the decisions are mine and mine alone. Do you understand?"

"Yes, Sir."

"Undress. Fold your clothes and put them on the table next to the chair." He leans against the counter and watches as I peel off my blouse and wiggle out of my tight skirt. I reach over and remove my pumps and set them on the floor in front of the table holding my clothes. I turn, hoping to see a reaction when he gets a look at my new lingerie.

"Fuck," he says with a smile. "I'll take those off myself. Get on the bed."

"Yes, Sir." I can't get there fast enough.

Slider stalks toward me, his hand slips around my back, and he unhooks my bra. Once it's gone, he leans over me and kisses my nipple. His tongue brushes back and forth before he nips the tip with his teeth.

"You're the sexiest thing I've ever seen."

"More." I groan and lift my chest in an offering.

He shakes his head at me. "I decide if you get more of anything. Hands over your head."

He puts one knee on the bed, reaches above me, and in seconds my hands are buckled together and secured to the headboard. Backing up, he surveys his handiwork, and then he takes a couple of pillows and slides them under my hips.

"The rooms here at Satin are reserved for a certain amount of time. I took this room out of the lineup for the night."

His smile is absolutely evil as he moves to the foot of the bed and slowly pulls off my stockings, kissing and nipping my flesh as he works. He hooks his fingers in the sides of my thong and slides it down and off my feet. His gaze sweeps over every inch of my exposed body. The heat radiating off him causes my pussy to pulse with need.

"Bend your knees and spread your legs."

With the skill and speed of someone familiar with restraints, each thigh is captured with a long strap and secured.

"Uh, Sir. I'm feeling a little exposed here."

His eyes darken by at least two shades. "Indeed. You are spectacular." Before I can comment, he's crawled up the bed and is staring at my sex. "Your scent is driving me insane."

His head lowers and he gives my pussy an open-mouthed kiss. His tongue plunges inside me, lapping my juices like a starving man. Had I not been restrained, I would have levitated. "Oh. My. God."

He lifts his head and props his chin on my mound. "You didn't make yourself come before leaving for the club, did you?"

"No, Sir."

His eyes narrow as if he's trying to decide if I'm telling the truth. "That's my girl."

Two thick fingers slide inside me, and his tongue finds my clit. I pull against the restraints, needing to bury my hands in his hair, to lift my hips and offer him all of me. His hand slides under me, lifting me off the pillow just a smidge but not allowing me any control.

"That's. . . that's." His fingers curve, pumping in and out against the spot inside that pushes me to the edge. "Please."

"No." Slider pulls away, and I almost call him a name I'm sure I'd regret. "Not without permission."

He stands at the foot of the bed and undresses. Taking his sweet time, he pulls his shirt loose from his slacks, one by one, undoes each button, walks to a chair, and drapes it over the edge. He reaches for the buckle on his belt, but he stops. He turns away and opens one of the drawers. I hear the cellophane crinkle as he opens something, then reaches for a bottle of what I think is lube and turns around.

I see the outline of his erection through his slacks, and he's hard as a rock, which tells me he's very much in control. He one-handedly takes off his belt and then stops.

"I need both hands. You don't mind hanging on to this do you?"

He walks back to the bed and sets the lube and a long narrow vibrator on my bare stomach before removing the rest of his clothes. His body is beautiful. Broad shoulders, narrow waist, with an extra dose of big dick, which is breathtaking. Then he climbs back on the bed and keeps crawling until his body is above mine. He kisses my forehead, my cheeks, neck, and then finally, he sucks one nipple into his mouth.

"Yes. God, yes." I feel him smile against my skin. He's having fun torturing me.

His hand massages one breast while his mouth and tongue play with the other until I'm writhing under him. My nipple is released with a pop, and he sits back on his heels. He picks up the vibrator and smears lube on it.

"Sir, I can't get much wetter."

"I know and I'm going to have my cock in that warm wet pussy soon. This is for your ass."

I feel panic bubble up in my chest. "I've never had anything foreign back there."

He lubes a finger and rubs it in a circle around my most private part. A second later his finger slides in easily.

"Oh," I gasp and tighten around him.

"Use your color." While he's talking, that finger is sliding in and out.

"Yes, Sir." The sensation isn't what I expected. He's found nerve endings I didn't know existed. My body responds, and I find myself wanting more. "Green."

"That's my girl." His eyes sparkle and that slight grin that makes him so damn sexy lights up his face. He adds a second finger and pumps in and out while his free hand picks up the vibrator resting on my stomach. "You're going to love this. Take a deep breath in and push it out when you feel the tip push against your sweet ass."

I swallow hard. "I trust you."

Slider pauses and his gaze meets mine for a minute. "I know and I'm honored."

His hand rests on top of my pussy. His thumb seeks out my clit just as I feel the pressure. It feels like a baseball bat as it slides inside me. He presses down with his thumb, and I almost come.

"You're doing great. How do you feel?"

"Full. Horney. I almost came."

"Don't do it. Not until I tell you too."

"What if I can't stop it?"

"Say yellow and we'll pause until you're under control."

"But. . ." I pull against the restraints.

"You're going to bruise yourself if you don't stop struggling." His tone is harsh, but then he leans down and licks me.

His tongue sends waves of pleasure to the tip of my breasts. "Oh, God."

"Good?"

"Yes."

"Then you'll love this." His tongue slides inside me just as the toy comes to life.

The vibrations in my backside and his tongue delving deep, lapping me like he's starving for the taste of me are too much. His mouth consumes me.

"Slider," I mutter his name over and over again.

The vibrator stills, and he quickly releases the restraints on my thighs. He grabs a condom from the counter and covers himself before climbing between my legs again. He pulls them up and over his shoulders. He grips his cock and slides it back and forth over my entrance. I swear my eyes roll back in my head when the bulbous head enters me.

"This is the last time a condom separates us." With those words, he shoves all the way in. His hips start to move, and a steady vibration flares up in my butt.

"Slider," I cry out as nerve endings threaten to explode in waves of pleasure.

"Come now."

****

A soft knock on the door brings me from a night of deep sleep to reality. I sit up, pulling the blanket Slider must have covered me with up to my chin. The first thing I notice is the vibrator is not inside me any longer. *Damn it.* I fell asleep on him. Again.

He's out of bed and is pulling on his slacks. He opens the door a few inches. I hear a female apologize right before he steps into the hallway and shuts the door.

A minute later he returns, and I can see the nerves in his jaw twitch. His eyebrows are pulled into a deep frown.

I get out of bed and slip on my panties. "What's wrong?"

He crosses the room, leans down, and kisses my forehead. "There's no reason for you to put on clothes. We're not going anywhere."

"So, nobody died?"

"Not yet." He scoops me up and crawls onto the bed with me in his arms. We land and bounce, the action pulling a laugh from us both. He slides off my thong, then his slacks, and tosses them on the chair.

Slider turns onto his side, props himself up on his elbow, and cups one of my breasts in his hand. His mouth captures my nipple, and he licks, sucks, and nips until I'm squirming. Then he switches to the neglected one. He lifts his head, and his fingers take over rolling and pinching.

His eyes are a dead giveaway. They glimmer with mischief. He leans over and nips my nipple. Pain and pleasure shoot through me. Endorphins flood my system, making me want things I didn't know I'd ever ask for.

Slider rolls over and grabs a condom.

"Put it on me."

"Yes, Sir." I can't wait to get my hands on him. I quickly cover him. "I'll be so happy when we don't have to use these anymore."

"Me too." His hands span my waist, and before I know what's happening, I'm on all fours with my ass in the air. He buries his face between my legs, and his tongue laps up my juices. "God, you taste good. Sweet and tart at the same time."

He owns my body, my responses, and knows exactly how to make me lose control. His tongue swipes my rear hole, and I almost collapse facedown. He chuckles.

"Soon, I'll take this virgin ass. When I do, you'll come harder than you ever have."

The head of his cock breaches my entrance, and I push back.

"You want more." He's teasing me, giving me a little at a time.

"Please," I plead.

He works his way deep inside me until his hips are against my ass. My mind loses touch with the outside world. We're all there is. Together, giving and taking. Slider moves slowly, his hand moves around, and his thumb runs through my juices. I tense when I feel him circling my anal opening. Around and around, until he applies enough pressure to slide inside.

"Color?"

"Green." I won't, can't, lie to him. "I'm good."

He leans over my back and kisses me between my shoulder blades. "That's my girl."

We start a new rhythm, me pushing back while he pumps his cock and thumb in and out of me. Pleasure morphs me into a person I don't know. I'm coiled like a spring that's about to come undone.

"Come for me." Slider's words barely reach my consciousness. "Now."

A sound rends the air, filling the room. It's me as I moan my release. My body collapses, and his strong arm comes around me, holding me up. He drives deep inside me, stills, and empties himself, pulsing again and again. He gently lowers me to the bed, rolling us on our sides, facing each other.

We're sweating and gasping for air, but we're smiling. He pushes my hair off my face.

"You're un-fucking-believable. I'm never letting you go. I'm keeping you."

I fight off the pressing urge to fall into a deep sleep. My hand cups his cheek. "Like a stray dog, you picked up off the street?"

"That's not what I meant."

"I'm joking."

"I wasn't." He kisses me. It's a soft and sweet touch of the lips.

I meet his gaze. His face has changed. It's softer, less intense. My heart swells in my chest. "I'd like you to 'keep' me."

"I didn't hurt you?"

"No. You showed me that sometimes a little pain brings a lot of pleasure." I can't hold back a yawn any longer. "Sorry. Sex with you knocks me out."

"So I've noticed." His lips curl into a satisfied smirk. He grabs a container of wipes and the cool scent of lavender glides across my face and neck. One by one, he tosses them aside until he finishes between my legs. "This time I'll turn out the light."

"Wait." I'd let the interruption pass without asking about it. "Who was at the door."

"Danielle. Vandals slashed the tires on my 'Vette and the limo. I told her to set the exterior alarms but not the interior ones. The tires will be replaced in the morning."

I pat the spot next to me. "Did the police come out?"

"No. Gabriel and I will watch the security tapes of the parking lot tomorrow. I have an idea who it was." He flips out the light and slides in bed beside me. His arm slips under me, pulling me onto his shoulder.

"You think it was the woman from earlier?"

"Rachel? Yes." His fingers run through my hair. "Rest before I get hard and take you again."

"Hmm," I whisper. Every muscle in my body is relaxed. I'm content when I feel the darkness pull me into a peaceful sleep.

Chapter 7

Slider

I sit in silence and watch her sleep for a few minutes. She'll be tired and possibly a little sore when she gets up. I woke her twice during the night, once turning her on her side and entering from behind, and then later I crawled between her legs and woke her with my mouth devouring her. She's so damn responsive, wet, and ready in seconds. I can't get enough of her. It's only our second time together, and I'm planning the next one and the next. I smile when an idea comes. I'll take her to the upcoming art show.

She turns over and her hand slides across the empty spot on the bed. "Slider?" She pushes herself up and leans back against the headboard. The sheet falls to her waist as her arms go over her head for a stretch. I'm reminded of a cat my mother had when I was a kid. Her eyes slide across me as she glances around the room. "You're dressed. What time is it?"

"Almost eight but you don't have to get up. I didn't ask when the repair truck would be here, but knowing Gabriel, it will be early."

She slides back down in the bed. "Do you have to be there?"

"Satin is my responsibility. I want to be there."

"You have a coffee pot behind the bar, don't you?"

"I do. I'll go ahead and get a pot started. It's not a Keurig, so give it time to perk."

Those long legs of hers slide out from under the covers. "May I watch the security footage with you?"

"Of course. You and I have no secrets."

"I like that." She stands, and I forget all about the flat tires.

"You are a beautiful woman. I could look at you all day." I laugh when her cheeks pinken and she glances away.

"I'm too tall."

"No, you're not."

"It's something I've been told all my life."

"What idiot told you that?" I stand, pick up her clothes, and take them to her.

"Too many to list. Different foster kids, a few fellow students, and more than one boy."

"They should have their asses kicked." I pick up her thong and hold it for her to step into. She laughs, and I want to make her do it again.

"Are you going to dress me?"

"Why not?" I lean closer and kiss the top of her mound. "There are benefits to being down here." My cell buzzes and interrupts me. "I'll be outside with Gabriel. There's a shower and a robe in my office you can use if you like."

"Thanks."

I pull her into my arms. "No more negative talk about yourself."

"Yes, sir."

"Text me if you need something. This shouldn't take long."

Leaving her behind causes an odd sensation in my chest. Even though we're in the same building, she's still learning her way around. The overhead lights power up, and I know Gabriel's in the building, so I make my way to the front and see him behind the bar starting the coffee pot.

"Good morning." He knows I've walked up without turning.

"Good morning." I smile when he faces me. His eyes are dark, and his lips are so thin they almost disappear. "Rough night?"

"I fucking hate this shit happened last night after I left. Zack called me and said Silken was crowded to the max and was shorthanded. I left here to go help him but returned after Danielle called me. It's time I expanded the security staff."

"You have four clubs under your umbrella. You can't be everywhere. Don't blame yourself. I damn sure don't."

"That's one of us who doesn't."

"Are you going to pour us any of that coffee?"

Gabriel does and brings both cups to the bar. His gaze sweeps me from head to toe. "You spent the night? That's a first, isn't it?" He grins and it eases the stern expression he always wears.

"Yeah." Interesting. I didn't give a second thought to staying overnight. "At least Kenzie's car isn't here?"

"You know Ty drove her?"

"Yeah." I slide onto a stool. "I told her to call him if she wanted to come out here." I frown at a thought. "Why didn't he let me know she was coming?"

Gabriel grunts something that sounds like a chuckle. "She's smart enough to charm your driver into picking her up and keeping it a secret so she could surprise you."

"He should've called."

"Ty agreed not to say anything unless you needed him and asked where he was. He told her he wouldn't lie to you."

I can't hold back a laugh. No woman has ever gotten under my skin like her. That she planned to arrive unannounced and the situation with Rachel ruined the surprise sits like a rock in my stomach.

"You getting attached to Kenzie?"

"I am." I catch myself grinning like a fool back at him.

"Good. She's a nice lady."

I lift the cup to my mouth and blow on the hot liquid. "I'm going to take her somewhere special next weekend."

"Where to?"

"An underground art show in Manhattan. I think she'll enjoy it."

"Give me times and dates. I'll make sure I'm here until you're back."

Gabriel's cell barks. "That's the tire guys. I told them this is a private country club."

I set my cup down and walk outside with him. Icy wind slams into me, reminding me I hadn't put on a coat. "Fucking snow in the forecast."

"It's not too bad." He's wearing a short-sleeve T-shirt and shows no sign of getting chilled. He shakes his head. "Go take care of your woman. I've got this."

"Is that your polite way of calling me a pussy?"

His laugher rolls across the parking lot. "I would never."

We stop at the limo first to survey the damage. Sure enough, all four rims are sitting on the ground. There's a couple of holes in each tire. "Fucking icepick."

"Looks like it to me." He leaves me to go talk with the men getting out of an extra-large truck with tires stacked on the trailer.

I jog across the lot to my car, stopping a few feet away. I'm not cold any longer. My blood springs to a boil as I walk around the Corvette. Tire flats are one thing but the scratches down the driver's side make me livid. I squat to get a better look at the door and easily make out the word *bastard* dug through the paint.

"Motherfucker." I turn on my heel and almost knock Kenzie down. I grab her arms and pull her against my chest and feel the knot in my gut unwind. How she restores my calm shocks me. "You shouldn't be out here. It's too cold."

"I'm fine. I found clothes in your closet to wear." She steps back and does a little curtsy.

I laugh. In the middle of the parking lot, I throw my head back and let go. She's wearing a pair of my warm-ups and a sweatshirt that could serve as a coat. "How are you keeping them from falling down?"

"That was easy. I borrowed a couple of your ties. Two pairs of your winter socks make decent slippers." She beams up at me with pride shining in her eyes.

"You learned how to make do with things a long time ago, didn't you?" I wrap my arm around her waist, and we walk to where the tires on the limo were already being replaced. "We're going inside. You good?"

"Sure. Sorry about your car."

"Yeah." I nod. "Me too."

"Want me to bring you a coat," Kenzie asks Gabriel.

"No, thank you. I'm fine." The corners of his mouth twitch. "You wear his clothes better than he does."

Kenzie and I go straight through to my office. My cell buzzes as we walk in, and I see it's work. "I have to take this."

She nods and walks to the far side of the room, looking at pictures of me, Zack, and Nick at various stages of our lives. I spend the next half hour working through a problem my IT manager is having trouble solving. I end the call and turn to find her on the couch with her legs pulled under her. She's so beautiful it makes my chest hurt.

"Hang on." I go pour us both a cup of coffee and return to my office. I hand her a mug.

"Thanks. Problem solved?"

"Yes. He could've handled it, but he panicked." I join her and she turns to face me. I lean down to her and capture her lips. They're cool and soft. "My mother would love you."

Kenzie's back stiffens, and I realize I've hit a sensitive nerve.

"Your mom probably has lots of stories about the trouble you got into as a kid."

I should've kept my thoughts to myself. "I hate that you didn't have a loving family growing up."

She pulls the corner of her bottom lip inside her mouth and chews on it. "I never talk about it. Not with anyone."

"I'm not anyone. I'm the man who wants to know everything about you." I won't push too hard, but I need her to trust me and not only in the bedroom. "You were six when you were placed in a foster home. Who took care of you before that?"

"My mom." Kenzie shrugs. "Truth be told, I took care of her. She was an alcoholic. When she came home alone, which was seldom, I helped her to bed. Cleaned up after her."

"You loved her."

"I wanted her to love me, but I was an albatross around her neck." Kenzie shrugs, and I see the pain as it flashes behind her eyes. "Her words not mine." Her gaze lifts above my head and she stares at the ceiling. It's as if she's watching a replay of her childhood. "There was an older couple in the apartment building who kept an eye on me sometimes." Kenzie huffs out a breath. "I remember being alone a lot. Maybe she forgot to tell them she was leaving."

I picked up on the "when her mom came home alone" and wonder about the times she wasn't. "She brought men home with you there?"

"Yeah. I hid in my room and stayed quiet. Sometimes they left pretty quickly but some stayed till morning."

"You still didn't come out?"

"No. I was too afraid."

"Where the hell was your father?"

"No idea." She shrugs as if it's of no importance. "I never knew him."

Fuck. My gut is burning. My chest feels as if there's a band around it and it's getting tighter by the second. "I'm sorry, baby. No kid should have to live that way."

"I still don't know how child protective services found out about us. It happened so fast that I don't remember it all."

"I've heard foster care isn't always a good place to be." I want to pull her into my arms and tell her nobody will ever hurt her again but now isn't the time.

"I was rebellious from the beginning. I was sure my mother would come for me. I was hurt and angry when she didn't. The longer I waited the more I rebelled and got in a lot of trouble."

"That's where the spankings came from?"

"Yeah. Some thought they could force me to behave. I was too stupid to appreciate that I had three meals a day."

Her chest is rising and falling a little too fast. I take her empty cup, set it on the table, and pull her onto my lap. "You went through a lot but look at you now. You're a brilliant, educated, and successful woman who can overcome any obstacle."

"I found a job when I turned seventeen and haven't stopped since. I remembered a teacher saying you had to have a plan."

"And you worked yours. I hope you're proud of yourself. I certainly am." Her body is stiff in my arms. I almost regret bringing up her youth. "I have a treat planned for us next weekend. Something I think you'll enjoy."

"Yeah?" Her interest shines in her smile. "What is it?"

"It's a surprise." A knock on the door ends our conversation.

I get up and let Gabriel in. "Everything squared away?"

"Yeah. You ready to watch the security feed?" He sits at my desk and starts clicking keys.

"Absolutely." I pull two chairs close so Kenzie and I can both see. Gabriel pulls the focus in tight on the area where the limo was parked and fast forwards the clip in small bursts.

"There," he says, freezing the screen. "Rachel."

Kenzie leans forward. Her head turns toward me with eyes wide as saucers. "Who carries an ice pick with them?"

"Good question."

"You have to turn the tape over to the police," she says.

"No. I'll handle this myself."

"Rachel belongs in jail."

I cover Kenzie's hand with mine. "What we do here isn't illegal, but the last thing we need is notoriety."

"So, you'll wait until she uses the ice pick on you?"

"Trust me. We won't see any more of her temper tantrums. Her father's an important man in town. Gabriel, you know who her father is, don't you?"

"Yeah." He smiles knowing what I'm thinking. "I'll make you a couple of copies."

"I've met him at different functions. He seems like a decent guy, so I'll take him a copy. If anyone can get Rachel under control, it's probably him." I stand and help Kenzie up. "You must be starving. I know I am. Let's get out of here."

"Go," Gabriel says. "I'll set the alarms and be out of here in ten minutes."

"Tell Danielle I won't be in tonight."

"Will do." He stands. Stopping at the door, he glances back and nods to Kenzie.

"Grab your things and I'll bring the car to the front door." I pull her face close and cover her lips with mine. *God, she tastes good*. Clean and sweet. Our tongues parry back and forth. That's all it takes for my cock to demand attention. It's with great reluctance, I lift my head and brush her soft bottom lip with my thumb. "Mine."

The drive to town is an easy one, especially mid-morning on Sunday. Kenzie is checking out the countryside, and she surprises me when she reaches over and puts her hand on my knee.

"You know about my childhood. Tell me about yours. I'm sure you were a handful."

"It doesn't get any more boring than my past. Both my parents are still living and together. Dad was a programmer when the video games industry took off. He must have created hundreds before he finally sold one. It wasn't for a lot of money, but it got his name out there, and soon he was doing quite well. When he turned fifty-five, he retired early, and they moved to Florida. I'm an only child, which probably explains why I want what I want when I want it."

"That's interesting, but what about you. What did you want to be when you grew up?"

"I have an uncle who was a Navy SEAL. I wanted to be like him as far back as I remember. I spent many years working out, running, swimming, anything to build strength and stamina. I don't think I really knew who I was until I committed to and then survived BUD/S training." Glancing at her and seeing her rapt attention makes me feel great. "I'm an average guy who made some good friends while in the Navy. When I got out, I made a few smart and lucky business choices, and they've paid off financially."

"Have you ever been in love?"

I glance at her. She's waiting for me to be honest with her. "I had a near miss. It ended when someone gave her money, a house, and kids."

"You don't want a family?"

"Not then. My commitment was to the Navy. Have you?"

She hisses out a sound. "I'm not sure I'd recognize it if it bit me in the ass."

I park, get out, and go around to help her. Her skirt rides up as she swings her legs around and puts her feet on the ground. I don't get a full view, just a peek of her pink upper thigh.

She's smiling. "I told you. I could easily flash someone if I'm not careful."

"That won't happen. If we're using this car, I'll always be between you and any audience that might happen to look." I take her hand and walk her to her door. "This is as far as I go today."

"You're not coming in?" The disappointment in her voice and on her face does my soul good.

"No. I have a couple of errands to run, but I'll call you before you go to bed."

"My alarm goes off at seven so maybe call early?"

"Seven? What time do you go to work?"

"Nine. But I jog every morning during the week."

"That explains those well-toned legs."

"They come in handy."

The memory of her legs locked around me has me getting hard. I pull her in and kiss her. Our tongues mate, dueling for more. She clutches my shoulders as if she doesn't want me to go. "How about I pick up dinner and stop by tomorrow after work?"

"I'd like that."

I place a quick kiss on her forehead and back up. "Go before I change my mind about leaving." She opens her mouth, but I cut her off. "Go."

She unlocks the door and steps inside but before I walk away, I tell her, "Don't make plans for the coming weekend. Remember, I'm taking you away."

Her face lights up like a kid opening birthday presents. "Where to?"

I shake my head. "Nice try. You'll never guess."

Chapter 8

I just barely get logged in at work before Madison is in my cubicle. "Good morning."

I smile, knowing she's going to grill me about Slider. "So how was your weekend?"

"Boring. How was yours?" She's staring at me as if the answer is written on my forehead.

"Dinner with a friend."

"The stalker friend named Justin?"

"He's not a stalker. He just happened to see us leave the building." I'm not sharing more information with her. The last thing he'd want is me chatting about our Saturday night together.

She leans against my desk. "Is he as good in bed as I think he is?"

"Madison!" My jaw drops at her question. I push back from my desk, stand, and glance around. Satisfied no one overheard her, I sit and open my email but can feel her behind me. "I'm not discussing my personal life at work."

"Then we'll do lunch." She pushes off my desk and disappears around to her side of the panel.

I've never had a close girlfriend. I learned early on that sharing secrets with housemates doesn't always stay secret. They can be used against you when the spotlight needs to be directed at someone else. I'm an easy target because it is usually me who causes the most trouble.

Putting the past out of my mind, I work through my emails, saving one from the junior partner telling me my research was exactly what he needed. I have two new assignments, so I print off the requirements, grab my laptop and cell, and head to our legal library. I isolate myself at a worktable in the back corner with the volumes of information I need and dig in.

After a couple of hours immersed in the law, my cell vibrates, pulling my attention away from work, but Slider's name on the screen makes me smile. I open his text and read.

Slider: *Having a good day?*

Me: *Yes. You?*
Slider: *Dull stuff. Can't wait to see you.*
Me: *Me too.*

My thumbs hover over the screen. How bold should I be?

Me: *I can't wait for tonight.*
Slider: *Good. I can't wait for dessert.*

My body heats up at his words. I glance around, and nobody is paying attention to me. The firm's law library is a busy place and most of the tables are full.

Slider: *Are you blushing?*
Me: *Of course.*
Slider: *Good.*

I start to respond but see the dots race across my screen, so I wait to see what's coming.

Slider: *Take off your panties.*
Me: *What? Now?*
Slider: *Right now.*

A million ants have taken residence under my skin.

Me: *I can't.*
Slider: *Take them off and leave them off.*

I leave my work on the table, go to the restroom, and close myself in a stall.

Me: *I'm doing it now.*

I slip off my bikini underwear and realize I have nowhere to hide them. Reluctantly, I tuck them inside my bra. This is the most outrageous, erotic, sexy thing I've ever done.

Slider: *Done?*
Me: *Yes, Mr. Impatient.*
Slider: *Good. I'm texting info on the closest clinic.*
Me: *K. It's lunch so I'll go now.*
Slider: *See you.*

I wash my hands and check my reflection in the mirror. My cheeks are flushed, and I'm breathing hard. Will anyone else see how turned on I am?

I make my way back to my worktable and find Madison waiting for me.

"Let's go downstairs to the cafeteria," she says. "I hear the lasagna is good today."

My cell buzzes, and I know it's the address of the clinic. "You go ahead. I have an errand to run." I grab my bag and make my way down the hall to the elevator. I check the address and am pleased the location is only a few blocks away. I cross the lobby and step out into the chilly weather. Damn, I forgot my coat in my cube. I jump when someone touches my shoulder.

I whirl as a suit coat wraps around me. "Slider!"

"Get in." He motions to the limo idling at the curb. "We can get blood drawn and then have lunch."

"You're awesome." I slide inside the warmth. The privacy window is up, and I wonder if Ty's driving.

"Are you just figuring that out?" Slider laughs, and my insides melt. "Ty's going to pick up lunch for us while we're in the clinic."

I breathe out a huge sigh.

"What was the big sigh for?"

"I was worried you'd be pissed at Ty and fire him."

"He didn't do anything wrong."

I lean over and cup Slider's face in my hands. His skin is warm under my fingers. "You're a nice guy."

"I know dozens of people who would debate that. Including my partners, who think I'm a whore dog."

"Well, they're wrong."

"So, you're an authority?"

"You're monogamous."

He grips the lapels of his coat around my shoulders and pulls me closer. So close our noses almost touch. "I am now."

The limo comes to a stop but before we get out, his hand slides under my skirt and his fingers brush my naked pussy. His growl makes me throb.

"Soon. You and me, skin to skin."

My mind flashes an image of him buried deep inside me without a condom. I open my mouth, but nothing comes out. *God, I hope I don't have a damp spot on my skirt when I get back to work.*

His smile is smug when he reaches around me, opens the door, and climbs out. He takes my hand and together we go inside.

The waiting area is full, and I take the last chair while Slider signs us both in. He hands the receptionist his credit card, signs the receipt, and returns to stand next to me. The woman behind the desk says something into her headset, and two minutes later we're being escorted to a back room. I'm thinking Slider called in a favor because we are in and out in just a few minutes.

Ty is waiting next to the limo and opens the door before we get there. The aroma of food greets me, and I hurry to get in the car.

A pizza box and a stack of napkins are waiting for us. "It smells heavenly in here."

Slider slips onto the seat across from me. "Hungry?"

A memory flashes and I close my eyes. "Yeah."

His hand closes over my knee. "What just happened?"

"Something from my past flashed through my mind. I remembered pizza being delivered but there wasn't enough for everybody."

"A foster home memory?"

"Yeah. I've eaten pizza many times since then. Why the memory surfaced now is confusing."

"Did you go hungry?"

"No. The slices were cut in half and we all got one."

"I'm sorry you didn't grow up with loving, doting parents. But your past made you who you are today and brought you to me, and I think you're perfect."

Tears slide down my cheek, and I quickly wipe them away with the back of my hand. "That's the nicest thing anyone has ever said to me."

"Get used to it." He takes a napkin and pats my cheeks dry. He picks up a second and tucks it into the front of my blouse. "Let's eat."

Two slices later, I'm full. I peek out the window and see we're parked in a no-parking zone. "I should get back. I'm in the middle of a new project."

"I'm sorry but I have to cancel dinner. Danielle called in sick. I need to be at the club."

"It's okay. I didn't quite catch up with my laundry yesterday."

"I'll make it up to you." He slides out of the limo, and I give his coat back to him as I get out. "Remember the surprise I mentioned?"

"I do."

"Friday after work, we'll fly to New York, do some shopping Saturday, and that night you'll see your surprise."

My excitement bubbles over, and I lift up and kiss him. "I can't wait."

"I'm having a couple of things delivered so expect a few packages."

"What's coming?"

"A dress and accessories."

Instant anger zips up my spine. "I can buy my own clothes, thank you."

"Whoa." He holds out his hand, palm up. "I want to give you this. Something special for a special night with my special girl."

"I'm used to taking care of myself, Slider. I pay my way."

"I know that, but you're not alone anymore." The nerve in his jaw twitches. "When a person cares about another, they like doing nice things for them. How is that wrong?"

I watch the different emotions flash across his face. I see that he's pissed, but there's hurt behind his eyes. "I'm sorry. Spontaneous gifts aren't something I'm used to getting."

His eyes narrow. "You'll have to get used to it." His words are harsh-sounding, but he leans forward and kisses my forehead. "I'll call you tonight."

I stand in the cold until the limo is out of sight. The icy wind blowing around my legs reminds me I have no panties on, so I dart inside. I enter the elevator and push the button for my floor. I exit and make my way back to the law library.

My work is exactly as I left it, so I pick up where I left off. I'm so aware of being bare under my skirt that it's hard to concentrate. Add that to having pissed Slider off, and I have to read everything twice. Every time I move in my chair, I'm reminded of him. I sense the moisture building and worry it's going to show through.

Finally, I get in the zone and concentrate. The sound of chairs sliding on the carpet, books being shelved, and voices pull my attention to my surroundings; it's time to go home. I put everything away, walk to the parking garage, and get in my car. I realize how much I'll miss Slider tonight.

The drive home is pure hell. Traffic is backed up, and I sit without moving for almost an hour. It gives me time to imagine all kinds of things. I should probably apologize to Slider for snapping at him. Maybe I'll just wait him out. It's too soon to care about him. I won't allow myself to look past tomorrow with Slider. Finally, I make it off the freeway and weave through the neighborhood until I reach my apartment.

I park and waste no time getting inside, where I kick off my heels and remove my blouse and then my skirt. Laughter bubbles up as I open the drawer where my underwear lives. Should I or shouldn't I put on a pair of panties? In the end, I remove my bra and slip on a long-sleeved T-shirt and yoga pants with nothing under them.

I take out a package of deli-sliced ham, a slice of cheese, the mayo, and make myself a sandwich. I grab a bottle of water and a bag of Cheetos before crashing on the couch. TV remote in hand, I scan channels until I find a rerun of *Law and Order: Criminal Intent,* and then I snuggle down to eat and let my brain go numb.

The buzzer alerts me that someone is downstairs. I set my dinner aside, walk across to the panel next to my door, and push the answer button.

"Who is it?" I don't normally have people who just drop in to visit, so I'm careful.

"Delivery for Kenzie Stone."

My day just got brighter. Slider's gift is here. He's not so pissed that he canceled it. "Come up and leave it at the door."

I pace until I hear the knock at my door. A quick peek tells me the delivery guy is gone so I open the door and find four boxes. Four! I take them inside and over to the couch.

My cell buzzes, and I know who it's from. I check and it's from Slider.

Slider: *Try everything on and let me know about the fit.*

Me: *K.*

I open the largest box first. The items are wrapped in white paper with the words *Saks Fifth Avenue* on them. Inside, I find two expensive-looking wraparound dresses labeled Ladybeetle by Zimmerman. *Oh. My. God.* My mouth dries up.

I text Slider.

Me: *I can't accept these dresses.*
I watch as the dots fly on my cell. He's responding right away.

Slider: *Yes, you can.*
Me: *They're too expensive.*
Slider: *You'll wear them this weekend.*
Me: *I will?*
Slider: *Yes. It pleases me to send you gifts. Talk soon.*

I pick up one of the dresses, and my hand smooths down the softest fabric I've ever held. It's violet-blue with waves of navy running through it. It has blouson sleeves and elongated cuffs. I have to try it on. I strip and slip it on, wrapping the ties around my waist. I go into my bedroom and spin in front of the full-length mirror. The material caresses my skin and curves. *How can something so simple look like a million bucks?*

I gather the rest of the boxes and carry them to my bed, where I take out the second dress. It's a wraparound also but more casual. The long-sleeved jersey in a paisley print is dressy but nothing like the first dress.

I open the smaller one to find two pairs of shoes. *How does he know my sizes?* The strappy four-inch heels are a lot for my height, but if it doesn't bother him, it won't me. I tear open the last box, thinking there's nothing left that will surprise me until I pull the formal gown from the box. It's a red Stella McCartney. My legs give out, and I sink onto the bed, holding the crepe material as gingerly as I can. I fight back tears as they build in my eyes.

I know Slider has money. But this is beyond generous; it's extravagant. Foolish. Touching. Thousands of dollars were spent on the clothes on my bed. My hands tremble as I stand and try on this masterpiece. The square neckline, spaghetti straps, and low-cut back look great on my body. It's as if it were designed for me. I would never have picked this color for myself, but it looks great with my complexion and hair. A daring slit reveals my right leg to my upper thigh. If I move wrong, I might show too much.

The fact no underwear came with the clothes doesn't escape me. Using great care, I remove the dress, do my best to put it back in its original state, and then do the same to the rest. Once I'm satisfied, I place everything back in the boxes.

I pick up my cell and text Slider.

Me: *I need to see you.*

He responds a few minutes later.

Slider: *I'm bringing dinner tomorrow night.*
Me: *Fine. See you at seven.*

I change my ringer to silent, grab a book, and stretch out on my bed. I need to figure this out. I can't let him spend this much money on me. The long gown alone would pay my rent for a couple of months. I need sleep but fear it won't happen.

Chapter 9

Slider

"Mr. Price will see you now."

I stand and follow the Cook County District Attorney's administrative assistant down the hall to the corner office. She taps the door and then opens it. "Mr. Locke."

Carlton Price stands to shake my hand, waves me to a chair across from his desk, and sits. "I don't believe I've seen you since the fundraiser for the addition to the hospital. What can I do for you?"

I lean forward in the chair and broach a subject that's sure to ruin his day. "I need your help with Rachel."

Price sits up straighter, and his eyebrows draw together. The warmth previously on his face vanishes. "Maybe you'd better explain."

I get straight to the point and am precise as possible while I explain my history with his daughter. I leave out the part where she and her ex-husband frequented adults-only clubs, only discussing Gallants and why I have a restraining order against her. I'm hoping I don't need to show him what's on the flash drive in my pocket.

"Saturday night, Rachel repeated her temper tantrum and destroyed tires in the parking lot. I decided not to call the police but to ask you to intervene. The last thing I want is more trouble, and I believe you may be the only one who can help. She's going to hurt somebody or hurt herself."

His shoulders droop. The fight is gone. "Rachel has been going through a rough period. I've asked her to get help."

"Insist. She violated a protection order by getting near me and then pulled a stupid stunt. I have cameras in the parking lot. They are irrefutable proof it's Rachel stabbing tires with what looks like an ice pick. I'm telling the truth when I say that I never, not once gave her the impression there was or could be anything between us. I truly don't want to make trouble for her. She needs help."

"I appreciate you keeping this out of the press. I'll see to Rachel."

I stand. "Thank you. Good luck in the election."

He gets up, rounds the desk, and shakes my hand. "I appreciate your discretion."

I leave the building with a small amount of confidence I've seen the last of Rachel. I don't need publicity any more than Carlton Price does. I get in my car and drive to a take-out restaurant close to Kenzie's apartment. With supper in the bag, I park in a visitor slot, get out, and make my way to the elevator.

I get off on her floor. I'm still a little pissed with her. I like that she has an independent streak, but if I want to do something nice for her, she'll have to accept it. I grew up with people doing thoughtful things for me. My family was and still is giving and considerate.

My knock is answered quickly. "I hope Thai is okay."

Her eyes flash wide as she steps back for me to enter. "It's perfect. Come in."

I put my briefcase on the coffee table and then place the sacks of food on her dining room table, then turn to face her. "Come here."

She doesn't hesitate. I tug her against me before clasping the back of her neck with my hand. Leaning down, I kiss those soft pouty lips of hers, wrap my other hand around her ponytail, and sink my tongue inside her mouth. Her soft lips are perfect. Perfect to kiss and to wrap around my cock. She's delicious and I worry I'll never slake my thirst for her.

There's nothing gentle going on here. It's all about lust and possession. Kenzie's nails sink into my back through my shirt as she gives as good as she gets. When I release her and step back, she gasps and pulls in a deep breath. I pull the results of my blood test from my pocket.

"My license to fuck you without a condom came via email today. Did you get yours?"

"I haven't checked my personal email since morning."

"Some people have to wait for days. It pays to have friends."

She hurries to get her cell. "Hang on."

I walk into her kitchen and start opening cabinet doors. I gather plates and silverware, then carry them to the table while she's checking. She's grinning when she joins me.

"Me too."

"Let's eat and then we'll celebrate."

She's glowing and grinning as she opens the refrigerator. "Want wine? I have a decent white."

"Sure." I empty the sacks and spread out the different boxes, opening each as I go. Chopsticks are in the bag, so I toss them to the center of the table. She skirts around me, goes to the fridge, and grabs the wine, then two glasses before we sit, and start filling our plates.

I pour and lift my glass in a toast. "Too good news."

"To us," she says softly.

I nod. "If you were shopping and spotted a Cubs T-shirt or jersey, would you think about me?"

Her eyebrows pull together in confusion. "I would. I know you're a fan."

"So, if you bought it for me, how would you expect me to react?"

"I see where you're going, and the two have nothing to do with each other. I wouldn't buy you a three-thousand-dollar baseball shirt."

"If you could afford to, would you?"

Kenzie leans back in her chair. "I don't know."

"As your Dom, it pleases me to do things for you. It doesn't please me that you kick up such a fuss. I've told you before I wish I hadn't agreed not to spank you."

A grin creeps across her face. "My Dom. I like the sound of that."

My cock jumps to life at her words. I want to undress her and lick every inch of her body. "Don't change the subject."

"I'm sorry I overreacted."

"That's putting it mildly. Tonight, we'll see just how much you enjoy orgasm denial." I finish my dinner and wait while she finishes eating.

We clear the table, and then I pour a second glass of wine for both of us. "Let's talk about this weekend."

She follows me to the couch and sits next to me. "Do you want to see the clothes you purchased?"

"No. I'd rather wait until you wear them."

"They are really very beautiful."

"I'm pleased that you like them."

"I love them." She lifts her glass to her lips and sips her wine. "I've never gone anywhere fancy dresses are required. Do I get a hint as to where I'll be wearing the evening gown?"

"We're going to an ice sculpture art show in Manhattan. It's a select clientele and by invitation only. I'll pick you up at six-thirty Friday, and we'll return Sunday sometime in the afternoon."

She swings a leg over me so she's straddling my thighs and kisses me. "Thank you." One kiss. "For the clothes." A second kiss. "For the trip." A third soul-searing kiss. "For understanding my weirdness."

"You're not weird, unique maybe, but not weird."

"I'm excited about the trip."

"I like watching your face light up when you experience something new." She rocks back and forth over my rigid cock.

"I've experienced a lot of new things since that first time I came to Satin."

"I want to be the one to show them to you." The minute I finish that sentence, I realize it's the truth. It's a truth I wasn't aware of until just now.

My fingers find the hem of her T-shirt. I pull it over her head and free her perky breasts. I sink my face between them, running my tongue over to one rosy nipple and then the other. She reaches between us and tries to unzip my slacks. I'll yield a lot of things to her, but who's in charge of sex isn't one of them. I slap her hand and lift her off my lap so she's standing between my knees.

"Sorry, Sir." She drops to her knees, lowers her head, and places her hands, palms up, on her thighs.

My chest tightens. "What is it about you that ties me in fucking knots?"

I'm not lying to her. She haunts my thoughts. I catch myself wishing she was with me whenever I see something she might find interesting. I had to hold myself back from calling and texting her from work last night. The club was unusually crowded and yet, my mind couldn't stay focused.

I've never had a problem fucking a woman and then walking away without a second thought. Sex is for enjoyment. I've always made sure my partner had as much fun as I did, but when it was over, I accepted it for what it was, a fast and fun release.

"I don't know what ties you in knots, but hearing that makes me happy."

"Look at me." I like that she dropped into position but need to see her eyes.

She smiles up at me. "Some Doms find the right partner and become monogamous."

I reach over and stroke her cheek. "Have you been researching again?"

"I might have spent a little time trying to learn more about the lifestyle."

"What did you learn?"

"Did you know what you eat can affect the taste of cum?"

"I did not." I stare into her wide innocent eyes for a second. "You're serious."

"I read it on a blog. She and her Dom experimented to see if it was fact or fiction and found it to be true. The comments were varied but a lot of them agreed."

"So now you want me to start eating strawberries every day?" I can't help but tease her.

"That's not what I said." Her cheeks are bright pink. "But I think I'll keep a variety of fruit on hand."

"Well, I love the way you taste, so don't change what you eat for me."

"I meant for both of us." Her cheeks flush bright pink.

I bite back a laugh. "I'm game." I rise and pull her up so she's standing.

"I want you upstairs and naked in bed in the next two minutes." I turn her toward the stairs and smack her ass cheeks. The second I make contact, I freeze. "I'm sorry. It was just a playful swat."

She glances over her shoulder at me and then takes off running. "I liked it," she calls out as she disappears up the stairs.

I reach for the briefcase and take it with me to her bedroom. She's stretching out on the bed just as I step inside. "You're so beautiful. I love your body."

"Thank you, sir." Her gaze drops to the case in my hand. "You brought work?"

"Toys." I set the case next to her and open it.

"May I?" Kenzie's eyes widen.

"Of course. They're either going on you or in you." I shuck my clothes as fast as I can while watching her hold up the nipple clamps and study them. "If I had to guess, I'd bet you've already researched those."

Pink rushes across her chest, up her neck, and paints her cheeks. "I may have watched a video or two."

"Good." I crawl up the bed and kneel between her spread legs. Leaning over, I crush her mouth with mine, licking at her until she opens wide. Her lips are soft, and she yields control. I sink in, and our tongues meet in a sexual dance. *Fuck, I love kissing her.* She's panting and grinning when I break away and return to the hardened peaks of her nipples. I suck hard, then back off and pinch and pull until she's squirming.

I take the clamps from her and place the first one on, tightening it a little at a time. Her gasp draws my attention to her face. "Color?"

She takes a couple of deep breaths while staring at her breast. "Green."

"That's my girl." I get the second one in place fast because I'll only leave the clamps on fifteen minutes this time.

"Oh. My. God. It hurts but feels good."

"You're fucking amazing." I slide farther down and lick the top of her mound. Her hips lift off the bed, and I bury my face into her offering. She tastes like heaven, sweet and tart, and mine.

"Yes. Yes," she groans.

"I love the way you taste." I fuck her with my tongue, taking a few seconds to lap at her juices before pushing as much of myself I can get inside her. Licking my way up to her clit, I circle the tiny bud, making each pass closer and closer to the prize.

I slide one finger inside her and pump again and again before searching for that bundle of nerves that will push her over the edge. I feel her walls clench, and the sound of her rapid breathing tells me she's close. I sit up and tug the thin chain connecting the clamps.

She lifts her head and scowls. "You're mean."

I laugh and laugh hard. "Oh, my darling, you have no idea." I roll her over and pull her onto her knees. "Head down." I slide a finger through her wetness. "Spread your knees."

"As you wish, sir."

"What a beautiful sight you present." My heart thumps hard against my ribcage as I crawl up behind her. Stroking my cock, I slid back and forth against her wetness. I sink my thumb into her heat, coating it with her juices, then circling her tight rosebud. Her ass tilts, pressing against the pressure I'm applying.

"Oh, God. Yes." Kenzie's words alter my original plan.

"You want me to fuck your virgin hole?" My brain is firing on all cylinders as I press inside her up to the knuckle.

"Yes. Please." She lifts her head, turning to look at me. "All of me belongs to you."

I back away, grab the lube from the briefcase and pop the top on it. My hand trembles as I coat my fingers and slather her tiny hole with it. Her body stiffens and I pause.

"I'm okay." Her whisper

I don't want to hurt her. I need her to love what I'm doing to her no matter what it is. I run my thumb in a circle around her tight entrance. She relaxes just enough for me to press one finger inside her. I slide it in and out until I'm comfortable she can take more. I add a second digit and scissor them.

Her words keep circling through my brain. She belongs to me. Trusts me. She's giving this intimate part of her that no one has touched before. Her moans and hip movements have me so hard it's almost painful. I want to slam myself inside her and pound. To let my inner beast ravage her ass hole, but I won't.

"There will be pain, but it won't last long. Use your safe word if you want me to stop."

"I want this. I want you."

I lean back on my heels and take a deep breath. Gathering my control and focus is important. No way am I going to ruin this for her by coming in the first few seconds. I exhale and move closer. "Take a deep breath and blow it out. Relax and let me in."

Chapter 10

Kenzie

I feel Slider's hand on my hips, his cock pressing against me. Pain shoots through me when the head breaches me. "Oh. My. God."

"That was the worst of it." His hands massage my ass cheeks, squeezing them and then spreading them wide. "I wish you could see what I see."

We rest in this position a second, and I realize the discomfort is easing. I test the sensation and push back against him. He growls. So, I do it again.

"You are so hot and needy." His hand strokes my lower back. "Fuck, you're tight."

"It hurts but you feel so good." I'm losing control. Giving myself over. I want the closeness of sharing something with him I've never done before.

"Jesus," he moans. Holding back has got to be killing him.

His hands grip my waist, fingers dig into my flesh, and then he eases his cock deeper inside me. My hand goes back to where we're connected.

His hand covers mine and slides it between us so I can touch our connection. "I'm all the way inside you. This feels incredible."

I drop my arm back to the bed. I feel so full and ready for more. "Fuck me, Slider. Please."

I cry out as he pumps in and out of me. There's no stopping now. He's in complete control of my body, and I love how his fingers dig into my hips. His thrusts get faster and faster. My orgasm rushes toward me.

"Slider," I cry out as nerve endings send fire shooting through my body. I feel his cock swell inside me and my mind blanks. "I'm going to come."

"Do it. Come with me. Now." His hand slides under me, his fingers find my clit, and he pinches it.

A tsunami of sensations slams into me, overwhelming me. I whisper his name again and again while I spasm around him. My body clutches and releases as I press against him while he's buried deep inside me. My climax hits with an intensity that seems never-ending.

Slider's hands tighten, holding me in place as his body stills against mine. His body jerks and the sound of his groans fill the room. His cock throbbing inside me pushes me to a second orgasm.

"Kenzie." His voice is raspy and soft. Releasing the nipple clamps, he leans over me and kisses a trail between my shoulders. "I'll be right back."

He slides from me, and I collapse onto my stomach. My brain is in a fog as I try to sort out my feelings. Maybe now isn't the time to dwell on how when we're together I'm the happiest I've ever been. The connection between us is much stronger now. More personal. More intimate.

A wet warm washrag pulls my attention back to the here and now. He's gentle as if he were handling fine china, and I stretch, almost purring under his care. He goes back to the bathroom, but soon he's next to me on the bed. He pulls me into his arms, rests my head on his chest, and then kisses my forehead.

"Thank you."

"For?"

"For giving me a part of yourself no one else has ever had. You trusted me completely and I'm honored. I will never give you cause to regret it."

I bite my tongue to keep from saying how much he means to me. It's not love. It can't be, not yet. But he's part of me now, and deep down I can't help but hope he cares for me too.

****

This week has taken forever to end, and my nerves are jumping like I've stuck my finger in a light socket. I still don't know much about this trip. Packed and ready to go, I'm so excited I can't sit still, so I pace and think about our lack of communication for the last three days. I fell asleep again Tuesday night after a late night of amazing sex. I admit to being a little disappointed when I woke up Wednesday morning to a note that he'd had an emergency at work. Hackers had infiltrated a customer's system, and other than a few hurried phone calls and late-night texts, we haven't been in contact. He promised that if he had to work twenty-four seven, our trip wouldn't be canceled.

I miss him terribly. Not just sexually, although I am getting spoiled by the number of orgasms he can give me in one night. I like talking with him, spending time together, even watching reruns on television is better when we're together.

My heart jumps when the knock on my door comes. My bag is by the door so when I open it, I won't delay our departure. My heart melts at the sight of his smiling face.

"Miss me?"

"God, yes." My arms curl around his neck. My body melts into him, and I'm whole again. My lips find his, and I slide my tongue across his lips.

The Dom in him rears his head, and he takes charge of the kiss. He pulls my hips close against him, and I feel his growing erection while his tongue assaults my mouth.

A growl rolls from him and he steps back. "I love that you're tall and how your body lines up perfectly with mine."

I glance down between us and then look up at his smiling face. "I like it too."

"You look beautiful in your new dress."

I step back and do a twirl, send the skirt sliding around my legs. "Thank you. It fits perfectly."

"Yes, it does." He adjusts himself and picks up my suitcase. "Your chariot awaits."

I wrap a scarf around my shoulders, and we make our way downstairs where the limo is waiting at the curb. Ty is leaning against the fender. The frown on his face is curious since he's always smiling. He pushes away from the car and opens the door.

"Something wrong?"

"That woman who just got banned from the club was here demanding to know who you were picking up tonight."

"You recognized her?"

"Yeah. Gabriel showed me her picture."

"That would be me." Rachel steps out of the darkness and casually strolls to where we're standing. Her eyes are locked on me. "You can go back into the hole you crawled out of, slut. The grownups have business tonight."

"Get in the limo," Slider says softly.

He's mine and I won't run from the crazy bitch. "He wants nothing to do with you."

Her eyes burn with insanity, and her mouth distorts into a sneer. "He'll never belong to you," she shrieks.

She lunges toward us. Slider's arm comes up and pushes me away. He slaps her hand, and an icepick falls to the sidewalk. He grabs her and pins her arms behind her and spreads his legs to keep her kicks from reaching him.

I hear Ty calling the police and Slider instructing him to contact Gabriel right away. My heart is in my throat, and I want to do something. Help in some way but don't know what to do. So, I stay out of the way, completely terrified.

"Tell him I want Rachel's father at the police station when we get there." Slider's tone radiates anger. His gaze swings to me. "You okay, love?"

No words will come, so I nod. My throat is clogged, and my body trembles.

"I've got her," Ty says. He takes Rachel from Slider and holds her in place.

The color drains from my face as he comes toward me. "You're hurt."

"I'm fine." He shakes his head.

"You're not fine. She stabbed you." Tears fill my eyes at the sight of blood staining his shirt.

Slider glances down at the crimson spot. "It can't be serious. I don't feel a thing."

"Let me see how badly you're hurt." I pull him into the limo out of the cold.

"It's nothing." He retrieves a first aid kit from under the seat, unbuttons his shirt, and inspects the wound. "A scratch."

"You need it looked at." My fear backs off and is quickly replaced by anger. "And that bitch needs to be locked away."

Slider cleans the scratch with a sterile wipe, rips open a bandage, and then presses it against his side. "I'm sorry she pulled this crap. Her sorry excuse for a father didn't step in and get her under control like he said he would."

"There's absolutely nothing for you to apologize for."

He smiles at me. "Don't get bossy." His wink tells me he's trying to lift my spirit.

"We should cancel our trip." Loud sirens blast away the silence. "The police will have questions for us."

Slider catches my face in his hands and kisses my forehead. "No, we won't. We'll be a few hours late but that's okay. We're still attending the art show tomorrow night."

His warm eyes and his touch have the most incredible calming effect on me. The way he handles everything in stride makes him even sexier.

The next few hours go by in slow motion. Police and ambulance vehicles arrive at the same time. Slider is immediately taken charge of by the paramedics. They inspect the small wound and put a new bandage on him.

Rachel is placed in the backseat of a patrol car and after the patrolmen speak with Ty, me, and then Slider, they haul her away.

Throughout the process, I keep Slider in my line of sight. I want to run to him and have him hold me close, but I don't. I wait in the limo because I know he'll return to me as soon as he can.

"Rough night?" Gabriel leans down, resting his arms on the roof of the limo.

"You could say that." I can't help but smile at him. He's so stoic I wonder if he has someone at home who makes him happy. "When did you get here?"

"Just now. Attempted murder isn't something Rachel will walk away from, not even with Daddy's influence. How's Slider?"

"The adrenaline has just about worn off, and he looked tired the last time I saw him."

"No doubt. I'll check on him."

I catch his wrist. "Thanks."

"My pleasure."

I lean my head back, close my eyes, and try to relax. Slider's fine and that's all that's important to me.

"I'm sorry, love." Slider gets in at the same time Ty takes his place behind the wheel. "We need to stop by the police station and give a statement before we leave. I'll try to make this as quick as possible." He puts his arm around my shoulder and pulls me close.

"How do you feel?" I reach to put my arm around his waist but stop.

"It's okay. The EMT said it would be sore but not to worry."

Ty drives away from my apartment and quickly gets on the freeway, heading toward the airport.

"You can't mean we're still going? You're hurt."

"It's a scratch, and the jet is warming up as we speak."

I stare at him. I know he has money, but he owns a private plane? "The jet? You own a jet?"

"The partners share it." His lips cover mine, cutting off any discussion. His kiss owns me. Sends me to a place far away from cold weather, crazy women, and shattered nerves. Here sensations and emotions rule.

****

I roll over onto my left side and stretch and snuggle deeper into the covers. It was after one this morning when we finally made it to the hotel, and I'm happy right where I am.

"You're awake. Good." Slider walks through the double doors into our bedroom at the Four Seasons Hotel.

I inhale the aroma of the coffee he's bringing me. It makes my mouth water. I push myself up onto the plush pillows and take the cup from him. I pat the bed next to me. "Thank you."

He's wearing warm-ups that hang dangerously low on his hips and no shirt. My eyes go straight to the bandage. "How do you feel?

"A little sore, but I've had worse injuries."

I take a drink of the hot brew and allow the caffeine to hit my system. "You're too good to me."

"Impossible. If you want to shower, there's probably just enough time before breakfast arrives."

I slide from the bed and stretch my arms overhead, completely comfortable being naked in front of him. "A shower sounds great."

Slider leans over and takes one of my nipples into his mouth and nips me with his teeth. He releases me with a pop. "Go. Now."

I hurry to the bathroom, pausing to look in the mirror. I look like a raccoon with a punk rock hairstyle. I stand under the water, letting the warmth loosen my tight muscles before washing my body and hair. I dry off and slide my arms into the fluffy white robe the hotel has provided and then I take special care with my hair and makeup before I join him. His back is to me, his head bent over the newspaper I assume came with breakfast. I slide my arms around his shoulders and kiss the side of his neck.

"Hmm." He lifts his head and looks at me. "You smell good enough to eat."

I groan and roll my eyes at his joke and then sit across the table from him. The view is spectacular, but my eyes drift back to his injury.

"That did sound a little cheesy." He shrugs those big shoulders. "But it's the truth." He refills my cup of coffee, hands it to me, and then removes the cover keeping the food warm.

I lift the cup to my lips and blow across the liquid. My eyes widen and my heart skips a beat when I spot a tray piled high with various fruit in the middle of the table.

"That's a lot of fruit."

The corners of his lips curl into an evil grin. He pops a strawberry in his mouth. "It's mainly for me."

I give up and let my laughter flow. "I'll eat my share."

He fixes a plate, loading it down with scrambled eggs, bacon, and toast. I'm surprised when he sets it in front of me. "That has to be yours."

He raises an eyebrow. "I've eaten. I'm just snacking now." He takes another strawberry from the tray, picks up the paper, and starts reading again.

The aroma stirs my appetite, and I tackle the food on my plate. While I eat, my mind wanders. I might take spanking off my hard-limit list. I don't believe for a minute Slider would take advantage of me. I've almost cleared my plate of food when he puts down his paper.

"It appears you were hungry after all."

"I must have been." I smile up at him.

"Why are you blushing?"

Damn, he doesn't miss a thing. "I didn't realize I was eating that much."

"That's not embarrassing. What brought on that flush on your cheeks?"

I open my mouth to deny it but think better of it. We promised to trust, and I'm going to try. "I was fantasizing about you spanking me."

Unadulterated lust fills his gaze. He looks at me for a long minute. "Thank you for telling me. Describe your fantasy."

I study his face. His eyes darken when he's aroused, and I know he's hard. My body wants to please him and be pleased by him. "I was across your lap, my bottom was bare, and you were spanking me with your hand."

He moves closer and opens my robe. His lips skim across mine on their way to my neck. "I smell your arousal. Just thinking about my hand on your ass and you're wet. Aren't you?"

"Yes, Sir."

"I can't take it off your hard-limit list yet. When you decide it's what you want, I'll be happy to make your daydream come true." His cell buzzes, and he takes a quick look. "We need to dress. Our car is waiting."

I'm so aroused he can smell me. If that's not embarrassing enough, he's not going to do anything about it. I shove my chair back, pull my robe together, and stomp toward the bedroom. A hand catches my wrist, turning me around. Storm clouds fill his eyes.

"Are you pouting?" His words are nothing more than a low growl. "Who's in charge of your orgasms?"

My throat catches. It's not anger I see in his eyes; it's disappointment. "You are. I'm sorry."

He turns away from me and walks to the closet where he hung his clothes last night. "Get dressed."

"I apologized." I slip on a bra and thong before taking my dress off the hanger. The material is butter soft and glides across my skin as I slip it on and secure it around my waist.

"And I accepted." His lips lift into a smile but it's not sincere. His eyes light up when he's happy and what I'm looking at is reserved. After he dresses, he glances at me. "Whenever you're ready."

He returns to the breakfast table. Picking up the newspaper, he snaps it open and starts reading again. My heart jumps to the back of my throat and tears fill my eyes. He's just taken a step back from me. I feel it in my bones. I can take him being mad at me but not disappointed. Somehow, my pouting set something off deep inside him.

I slip on my shoes, grab my cell and bag, and hurry to join him.

"The dress is beautiful." I do a little curtsey for him. "I can't thank you enough."

Slider folds the paper and drops it on the table. "We'll get you a coat first thing."

Four people are on the elevator when we enter, so there's no conversation as we descend to the lobby. I can sense he's not as tense as before, but it doesn't ease my fear.

He asks the concierge to let the driver know we're ready, and we walk to the exit and wait. Stepping outside is a shock to the system as the wind cuts right through me. I shiver and waste no time getting in the back seat of the town car. There's no divider so personal conversation is out.

I turn my head and stare out the window. Tears rush to fill my eyes, but I fight them back. Like it or not, I'm in love with Slider. I can't picture myself without him in my life. My bed. My heart.

Chapter 11

The realization Kenzie is struggling to let me lead is disappointing. The second thing I realize is how much I care for her. My chest tightens. This is an emotion I never expected. Never planned on having. Never thought one woman could satisfy my needs. Never. Until her.

Kenzie is independent, self-reliant, and smart. The word *mine* keeps circling back to the front of my brain. I need her, and my need is not just sexual. I need her smile. Her laughter. Her bravery.

The driver stops at the best winter-wear shop in Manhattan. He gets out, walks around to the sidewalk, and opens my door. "I can wait here or park in the garage across the street. A text will have me here to pick you up in five minutes."

"Wait for us. We'll only be a minute." I help Kenzie out of the car into the chilly air. The wind swirls around her legs, lifting the hem of her dress and then dropping it. I wrap my arm around her shoulders. "Let's get you inside."

One step through the door, she stops in front of me, and I almost run into her. She turns and with eyes wide, says, "We're not shopping here."

I take a deep breath. "We'll discuss this later, but for now, you will stop arguing with me."

"Sorry." Her head lowers and so do her eyes.

"This is my fault. I thought it was because I haven't been firm enough. Maybe it's going to require a lot more patience." I use my index finger and thumb to lift her head. "Look at me when we're in public unless I have told you otherwise." I turn her and we walk deeper into the shop.

Mr. Locke?" The woman walking toward us smiles.

"That would be me." I nod politely. It doesn't matter how much money I have or will have, being patronized because I'm wealthy pisses me off. "We're here to pick up Miss Stone's coat."

"Of course. If you'll follow me."

Kenzie's small hand slides into mine. I wink at her, and I lock our fingers together.

It's too easy for me to forget this is all new to her. My lifestyle, wealth, and demands must be alien. She's been independent a long time and yielding control must be difficult. I have to stop assuming she'll acquiesce easily.

The sales clerk excuses herself and disappears through a door, returning seconds later with a couple of coats draped over her arm. Instantly, Kenzie's fingers tighten on mine and her body stiffens. Her lips are tight and narrow, but she tries on three selections. Each time she shakes her head. I finally decide for her.

"We'll take this one." I pay for it and carry it in my hand. "Thank you. We'll show ourselves out."

The clerk's confused expression says it all. "Enjoy your stay in Manhattan."

I don't release Kenzie's hand when I turn us and walk to the front of the store. We stop and I try to drape the coat over her shoulders. She steps away from me then turns. The frigid gleam in her eyes stops me in my tracks. I've never seen this expression on her before. It's full-out anger. The kind that makes me think she hates me. My blood pressure shoots up, and I think my brain is frying.

"We had this conversation."

She doesn't blink. There's no look of apology or submission on her face or in her posture. "Red."

"What? You're using your safe word over a fucking coat?"

"I'm not wearing animal fur." Tears fill her eyes. "Not even for you."

It takes a second for her statement to register. "I would never ask you to. Demetri sells the best faux fur in New York." I take her hand in mine, tugging her out to the sidewalk, and point at the sign over the door. "Some of the biggest celebrities shop here."

"Oh." Her lips form the perfect O as the tears finally breach and trickle down her cheeks. She shivers against a blast of frigid wind that lifts her skirt almost to her hips.

I don't hesitate. I wrap her in the full-length fake mink and help her inside the car. "We need to communicate better. This fuckup is on me."

"I didn't read the sign." She burrows into the coat, pulling the collar tighter around her neck. "I'm sorry for thinking you would buy real mink."

"Me too, but I'm ready to put that fiasco behind us. Let's have an early lunch. There's a restaurant with a view you'll love. I want to show you." I reach over, stretch her seatbelt out to encompass the coat, and then fasten it just as the car moves forward.

"Absolutely." She crooks her index finger for me to come closer. "If we weren't in this limo, I would properly thank you."

"I'll remember that." I lean back, knowing there's no way I can let her go. She's mine, and if she wants me bad enough, we can work through our problems. We have to.

"Hey." Her hand squeezes my knee. "Where'd you go?"

"Sorry."

Her grip tightens. "Please don't give up on me. I've spent quite a few years protecting myself. When I told you I've never had anyone to depend on, it was the truth. I'm trying to give you one hundred percent control. Really."

"I don't want a robot who only does or thinks what I tell it to do. I want a commitment to be part of your life. The part that includes a Dom. Me."

"I want that too. We're great together." She studies my face. "Aren't we?"

I lift her hand to my lips and kiss the underside of her wrist. "We're better than great."

The limo stops in front of the Manhatta, one of New York's finest restaurants overlooking the East River, Brooklyn, and the Manhattan and Brooklyn Bridges. I get out and escort Kenzie inside to the elevator that takes us to the sixtieth floor. I love exposing Kenzie to new sights and showing her off at the same time. She's the most beautiful woman in the room, and it doesn't go unnoticed by the other male diners.

Seated next to the window, she sighs as her gaze takes in the dazzling cityscape.

"I'll bring you back here someday after dark. The view is breathtaking."

"It's fantastic. Seeing the city from up here is mesmerizing."

Our lunch goes as expected. The food is great and the service excellent, but it's Kenzie's enthusiasm with each bite that makes everything shine. I almost hate to whisk her back to the hotel.

Our ride drops us off in front of the hotel, and we join a family on the elevator getting off on our floor. Once inside the suite, she slides the coat off and carefully lays it across the couch arm. Turning toward me, she positively glows. She pulls her shoulders back and lowers her head.

"May I make an observation?"

She's already told me how she plans to thank me, so I let her wait for a heartbeat and then answer. "Go ahead."

"I was rude and almost caused a scene at the coat store. I sounded untrusting and ungrateful." She pauses and takes a deep breath. "I deserve to be spanked."

I don't know what I expected her to say, but it wasn't that. I take a minute to think about her statement. How much of me can I change if I want to keep her. I'm not sure it's even possible, but she's taken over my heart, and the thought of losing her is too painful. I want to take her in my arms and tell her everything is all right, but it's not.

"I'm not disciplining you until I'm convinced you understand what it means to be a sub and want to live that way."

"I want to serve you."

"That's a slave, and I don't want one. But being my sub isn't strictly sexual. It's about respect. When a sub is with their Dom, every thought they have, step they take, word they speak should demonstrate how much they value him or her. A sub surrenders their safety, well-being, and pleasure without reservation because they know—trust—their Dom always has their best interest in mind and heart at all times. As your Dom, I won't take that responsibility lightly. I will honor and appreciate you granting me the privilege." I place my index finger under her chin and lift it so she can look me in the eye. "I want this relationship to last. You have to commit, or we won't survive."

She opens her mouth, but I shake my head. "Go rest for an hour before we have to get ready for the art show."

"Yes, sir." Kenzie turns and slowly walks into the bedroom.

I watch as she slips out of her dress and heels, crawls under the covers, and rolls to her side. There's nothing I want more than to follow her into the bed and spend the next hour lavishing affection on her body. Instead, I wait until she's settled to walk over and pull the double doors closed.

****

Kenzie

Soft kisses on my forehead wake me. I roll onto my back and open my eyelids a crack. Pale blue eyes are looking down at me. *Should I tell him I'm falling in love with him? Would it scare him away?* I cup his cheek in my palm. His thumb strokes the blood vein pulsing in my neck. "I want you to know I won't turn into a Rachel if this thing between us doesn't work out."

He smiles, and this time, his eyes light up. "I know that, and I don't see an end for us any time soon. I don't want you worrying about that. We have a fun evening ahead of us. Let's enjoy it." He stands, offering his hand. "You need to get ready."

I rise and lean into him. His lips cover mine in a slow, soul-searing kiss. My chest aches as if it will crack open and spill my feelings to him. He hardens against me and I almost purr. His hands wrap around my forearms and push me back a step.

"Go." The blue in his eyes has darkened to navy. "Or we'll spend the night right here."

"If it would please you."

"It would, but we're not missing this art show."

I race to the bathroom, take my shower, and wash my hair quickly. I take extra time on my hair and makeup. My dress deserves the best presentation I can give it. I slide it on and let the rich feel of the material caress my skin. I love that the color enhances the red in my hair and hope he does too. Not having a bra or panties underneath sends sparks of desire south. I shake it off, straighten my shoulders, and, carrying my shoes, I walk into the main room of the suite where Slider is waiting.

His head is bent over his cell, and I take a second to appreciate how gorgeous he is wearing a tailored black suit and crisp white shirt. I grab my phone and snap his picture.

He senses my presence and lifts his head. The smile on his face means more to me than all the money in the world.

"You are so beautiful."

"Thank you again for the dress. I love it."

He stands and pats the seat of the chair he just vacated. "Come sit."

I follow his instruction. Walking slowly to the chair gives the full effect of how the dress clings to my body. I ease down, and the warmth from where he's been sitting meets me.

He takes my shoes and drops to one knee in front of me. His hand caresses the bottom of my foot, massaging my instep before slipping on one shoe. I feel like Cinderella as he repeats the process on the other foot. His smile is positively evil as his fingers inch up my bare leg.

"No bra. No panties." It's a statement, not a question. My legs open slightly of their own volition.

"This dress is lined but if you keep that up. . ."

"You're right. The last thing I want is to ruin your dress. Stay here." He stands and walks behind me. Something cool slides around my neck, and I put my hand on it. "Pearls? You didn't."

"The minute I saw them, I knew they were for you. The dress and pearls highlight your beautiful face and hair."

I open my mouth to protest, but my heart is so full of emotion, I can't speak. He gets my new coat and holds it for me to slip into. "Thank you for everything."

Slider moves the hair off my neck and places a soft kiss there. "You're very welcome. The car's waiting."

I can't help but notice other couples watching us as we work our way through the hotel to the concierge's desk. Slider is without a doubt the best-looking man in the building. His broad shoulders and chest are highlighted in the black suit. He's not wearing a tie, but that doesn't take away from his appearance. Every inch of him says male, money, and confidence.

I snuggle deeper into the coat and brace for the wind but find it's finally died down. The night air is still cold. Slider waves the driver off, seating me himself. He leans across and fastens my seatbelt, pausing to kiss me on the way. I catch myself following him as he pulls away, closes the door, and goes around to get in on the other side.

Our driver negotiates traffic like a pro, and soon we're traveling away from the lights of downtown to a dark warehouse district. Rows and rows of massive distribution centers fill the industrial park. When he stops and we get out, I can't help but notice the expensive cars and a couple of guards positioned where they can keep watch.

Slider takes my hand, and we climb the stairs of a plain, unmarked building. I turn my head to find him watching me. My trust in him is one hundred percent, and I can demonstrate it by not asking questions. That doesn't stop my curiosity or imagination. *Is this an art show or a BDSM club?*

"Nervous?"

"Not in the slightest." I laugh at his raised eyebrow. "Not with you next to me."

He kisses my forehead. "Good answer."

He presses a buzzer, and a man opens the door. Slider reaches inside his coat and pulls out an envelope. He passes it to the guy and waits while he removes a card. A moment later a smile appears on the guard's face.

"Welcome. Please enjoy yourself. Mr. Granger is expecting you. You'll find him with the other guests."

Slider helps me out of my coat as we enter and hands it to a young woman waiting just inside. He escorts me down a hall, opens a second door, and we enter a huge room.

"Oh. My. God." My brain tries to take it all in at once, but it's impossible.

"Corbin Granger is the premier ice sculptor in the world. He only holds this special showing once a year."

The walls are covered in what looks like red velvet and there are tables with chairs, couches, and a long bar covered with food. But there's a room within a room here. The sculptures are made of ice and are in a room made of glass. I hear the low rumble of refrigeration that keeps the sculptures frozen.

The first one is a sex scene of a woman pleasuring a man. He's buried inside her mouth and she's looking up at him. "Oh. My. God."

Slider snugs me against his side. "You already said that."

"It's so realistic. How on earth does he do that?"

"He has a rare talent. Let's circle the display."

As we move slowly around the room, trays of champagne carried by scantily dress women and men circulate. My nipples harden as my nervous system overloads when each carving seems to be more erotic than the last. We see displays of different sexual positions between men and women, men and men, and women and women, plus a couple of three-ways. Between each one is a small table with examples of modern and antique sex toys. This one has an ice riding crop resting next to an ice dildo.

"I read that wood and glass were used to make dildoes long ago. How safe was that?"

"Like all things, if properly prepared I'd think they got the job done." Slider's not looking at the display. His gaze is on my breasts. "You're not disappointed? Were you expecting to see Picassos or Rembrandts?"

"This is much better."

Slider moves behind me, his hands rest on my waist, and his erection is pressed against my ass. "Yes, it is. I particularly like the ice dildo."

I gently rub against him, loving that with my height and these shoes his erection fits perfectly between my butt cheeks. The next sculpture is a man using a dildo on a woman. Her head is thrown back, her mouth is open, and I swear she looks lost in ecstasy.

Slider steps back and takes my hand. "Let's find Corbin."

We move away from the glass room and into the small crowd of people. I'm surprised to see a few couples having sex. "They got so turned on they couldn't wait. That's quite a testament to the artist."

"What a nice thing to say." The voice comes from behind us.

"Corbin." Slider turns us, releases me, and pulls the small man into a hug.

"Justin, I'm so excited you came." His gaze swings to me. "Did you bring me a present?"

"I don't share." Slider's arm wraps around my waist possessively. "Sweetheart, this is the genius you were just talking about, Corbin Granger. Corbin, Kenzie Stone."

"Nice to meet you, Mr. Granger." I extend my hand.

He takes my fingers and lifts them to his lips, kissing each one. A low growl from Slider has him releasing me. I love he's showing signs of jealousy. It's the first time, and I'm over the moon happy.

A woman's cry stops the conversation, and the three of us turn toward the sound. We also laugh at the same time. Her back is against the wall and her legs are wrapped around her partner's hips.

I take this time to really look at our host. He's short, maybe five foot five. His gray hair is tousled as if he forgot to comb it, and while his suit fits as if tailored, he's wearing scuffed tennis shoes.

"If you'll excuse me, I see someone who does share."

"Of course." Slider grins and shakes his head.

The artist kisses me on both cheeks. "I have a gift at the door for you when you're ready to leave." He pats Slider on the arm and then shuffles away.

"Wow. He's quite a character."

"He's quirky and talented enough to get away with it." Slider's speaking to me but his eyes are still on the couple against the wall. "Let's finish the tour. If I see one more couple having sex, we may join the trend."

We grab another glass of champagne from a passing waiter and go back to the exact spot where we stopped. The sculpture is a woman straddling what looks like a saddle without the stirrups. Her mouth is open as if she's enjoying herself. A male is sitting and watching. "What is that?"

"It's a Sybian. In real life, it's electric. Some come equipped with two cocks some just the one. The submissive straddles it, seating the dildos in the appropriate orifices, and the Dom controls the remote and orgasms."

"Well, I certainly missed that when I researched."

His chuckle heats me from the inside out. "There's a room at Satin with more than a few things you might not have seen when you Googled BDSM. I'll make sure that it's marked reserved when you're ready to experience everything in it."

I look up at his face and see desire darken his eyes. "I'd love that."

His knuckles stroke my cheek. "Talk to me. What just happened?"

"Have you ever taken this much patience with a sub before?" I want the question back as soon as the words spill out into the universe.

"There I go again. Forget I asked, it's none of my business." I walk away from him, hoping he didn't see my embarrassment and pretend to be interested in the next display.

The last sculpture is a massive piece of work. It's erotic but so intricate in detail it's stunning. A woman on her hands and knees with one man taking her from behind and the other using her mouth. It's the expression on the female's face that makes my legs rubbery. Her gaze is locked on the male's face, and I swear I can see her eyes smiling.

I sense Slider as he moves closer. His hand slides around my hips, and I feel the hem of my dress rise as he pulls the slit in the skirt high enough his hand easily slides across my bare skin and between my legs. One finger is touching, rubbing circles, and then slipping between my folds.

"Did I mention how much I like that you're tall? Your pussy is so easy to reach." After slicking his finger through my wetness, he presses hard against my clit.

"Oh, God. That feels good." My head rests back against his shoulder. I breathe in his scent, close my eyes, and yield control. His finger moves faster, and his free arm snakes around my waist, holding me in place.

Our surroundings fade as I move closer and closer to the edge. My hips move, grinding against him, racing toward my orgasm. Suddenly, his hand leaves me, and I moan loudly. Embarrassment slams into me. I glance around and nobody seems to have noticed.

He smooths my dress down over my hips. "I can't wait to get you back to the hotel and see what gift Corbin is sending home with us."

"Why did you stop?" It hits me I've just been disciplined. I take a deep breath, let it out, and turn to face him. "You are in charge of my orgasms."

His eyebrows lift, and a small smile tugs at the corners of his mouth. He offers me his arm, and I clasp his bicep. "Let's find Corbin and say goodnight."

"I think that's an excellent idea."

We collect our gift, step outside, and wait for the car. "No. I've never taken this much patience with anybody before you, but then, I've never felt anyone was worth it until you."

Chapter 12

I hold the door open to our hotel suite and Kenzie hurries inside with the small gift box clutched to her chest. Corbin had written her name on the tag, and the guard at the door gave it to her on our way out. She's been dying to open it since we stepped outside of the warehouse.

"Now?" Her eyes sparkle like the sun ricocheting off the ocean. "This is so exciting."

"You've had presents before haven't you?"

"Some." She shrugs her shoulders.

Her answer is like a fist to my gut. "Some?"

"It's not important."

"How many are *some*?" I repeat.

"I can count the number of presents I've been given on one hand."

My breath catches. My fucking chest hurts. No one ever gave her a gift out of love? It's no wonder she didn't know how to react when the dresses arrived. I take her coat and drop it on a chair.

"Go for it."

My beautiful girl sits on the couch and slowly slides a finger under the tape holding the red foil wrapping paper in place. She grins at me before she opens the plain brown box. Inside she finds a couple of ice packs. She moves them aside and discovers her gift. Her laugh lights up her face as she holds up a vibrator.

"It's cold." She holds it out for me.

I take it, turning it in my hand. "It's safer than using an ice cube during sex. Remember the story of the little boy who got his tongue stuck to the flagpole?"

"Yes." Her eyes widen. "I can see where you'd have to be careful."

I extend my hand and help her up. "I suggest we put this to good use before it loses the chill and becomes an everyday vibrator."

I follow her to the bedroom, reach her side, and unzip the dress, pushing the straps off her shoulders. She shimmies and the gown falls at her feet. Toeing off her heels on the way to the bed, she stops and turns to face me. Naked except for the pearl necklace, she's the most beautiful thing I've ever seen.

"Fuck." My gaze rakes over her curves. My body aches for hers. Aches to push her limits. Aches to make her beg for more.

Before I can speak, she drops to her knees, lowers her head, and tucks her hands behind her back. I bend over and stroke her cheek. I walk behind her, taking myself out of her line of sight. I undress and open my shaving kit, removing a tube of lube and nipple clamps. When they're on the nightstand next to her new toy, I return to her, placing my hand on her shoulder to let her know I am next to her.

"Get on the bed, love." Calling her love is becoming a habit. I'm surprised how the word rolls off my tongue. It doesn't make me uncomfortable at all.

I join her, pulling her to me, I cover her mouth in a demanding kiss. Her hands tunnel in my hair, fingernails digging into my scalp. I move between her legs, and she spreads wide to accommodate me as I nip and then lick the pulsing vein in her neck. I sit back on my feet and just look at her.

"You are the definition of sexy."

"Thank you, Sir. I'm glad I please you."

"Everything about you pleases me." I take her soft breasts in my hands, massage them thoroughly before pinching her nipples between my thumb and finger. I roll them tighter, pull them, stretch them until she's writhing underneath me. Tonight, I'll push her further than ever before. I reach over and pull the clamps to where she can see them, showing her the little chain connecting them. "These are a little different than the first pair we used."

"They're beautiful."

"They're going to look beautiful on you." I twist one nipple again until it is rigid and then attach one clip, tightening slowly. After repeating the process on the other side, I lift up and study her. "Color?"

"Green, Sir." Her breathing is rapid, and her pupils are dilated.

"I'm so fucking proud of you." I tug the small chain. Her moan goes straight to my cock. "Breathe into the pain."

"I'm good, Sir."

I work my way down to her mound, stopping to French kiss the very top of her pussy, before spreading her with my thumbs and flattening my tongue to lick her back to front until she's squirming and moaning. "Roll over, love." Damn, I like saying that out loud.

I take the lube and work her tight ass hole until I have three fingers inside her, and she's pushing against them. "This ass is mine too."

"Yes," she says in a whisper. "If it pleases you."

"It does." I reach for the vibrator, which we'd left resting on one of the ice packs. It's cold to the touch when I slip just the tip of it inside her already soaked pussy. She jumps but I place my hand on her stomach and hold her in place. I slide it deep, pumping it in and out. She moans and lifts her hips.

"Oh. My. God. I already need to come."

"No," I snap at her. "Not yet." I lube my cock and line it up with her tight hole. I slowly push the head inside her. She clenches me like a vice. "Breathe out and push against me."

I hold myself in place until I feel her relax the stronghold on my cock. This is a slow process, but I want her to enjoy it. I'll do anything to not cause her pain. I keep pressing, inching my way until at last, my hips are flush with her butt cheeks, and I turn the icy vibrator on low.

She yelps. "Oh, my God."

I slowly pump in and out of her tight channel while moving the cold vibrator at the same pace in and out of her pussy. When she moves in time with me, I know we're good. "Still green?"

"Yes. Yes. I'm so full."

She's pressing back against me, meeting every thrust. The need to flood her with cum, to mark her as mine is powerful, but I fight back my orgasm because her pleasure comes before mine. She owns me, but she just doesn't realize it.

"Slider. Oh, God. Slider. Yellow. I can't stop it."

I stop thrusting and turn off her new toy. "Yes. You can." I remain still for a minute to regroup, and I then start moving again. I reach under her and tug the chain. "Color?"

"Green. Please, let me come."

My balls draw up, and I feel the warning tingle in my spine. Soon, I won't be able to hold my climax off.

"Please," she begs. "Harder. I need more."

"I start pounding in and out, pushing her closer and closer to the edge. She's moaning and pushing back, matching my every thrust. I reach around her, removing one clamp and then the other. As blood rushes to her nipples, I grant her request.

"Come now, love. Come with me."

She buries her face in the pillow. Her body thrashes under me and jumbled words spill from her lips while we come undone together.

I roll to my side, bringing her with me. Once she leans back against me, I reach around her, remove the vibrator, and then gently rub her sore nipples.

Neither of us speaks until we've stopped gasping for breath. She rolls to face me. Her eyelids are heavy, and the smile she gives me speaks volumes.

"Good?" I ask, kissing her forehead.

"Great." A dark cloud seems to slide across her eyes, and she quickly turns her back to me.

"What is it? Did I hurt you?"

She shakes her head.

"That won't cut it. Use your words."

Again, she shakes her head. I push myself up, lean against the headboard, and roll her to her back. Panic fills my chest. The tears leaking from her eyes and the absolute devastation I see in them rip my heart apart. I pull her onto my lap and gather her in my arms. Time passes and I can feel her body relax. I can't, won't, take my arms from around her. I need to be her shelter. Her home. *Fuck*. I need her to love me.

"Slider?"

"Yes, love? Can you tell me why you're upset?" I'll give her anything she wants. Do anything she wants. Say anything she wants, except goodbye.

"Not upset. Moved. I've never felt anything that powerful before. You took me somewhere I've never been. Thank you."

"It was my pleasure." I tighten my hold and rock her like a baby. I don't know how long we stay like this, but she finally sits up and turns her head so she can look at me. "Yes?" I ask.

"Want to hear something funny?"

"Sure."

"I don't remember ever being rocked before."

My chest almost cracks open. I push her soft hair off her face and over her shoulder. "Get used to it. I'm buying an oversized rocking chair and plan on holding you on my lap a lot."

She smiles up at me. "Really?"

"And for a long, long, time."

"I'd like that."

"I'm keeping it at my place. Our place if you'll come live with me."

She twists, slings a leg over me, and straddles me. Her body deposits what's left of my cum inside her on my bare stomach, bringing a soft giggle from her. The tears are gone. They've been replaced by a smile spread across her beautiful face. "I'd like that too."

"Come down here."

She leans forward, and I reach around and smack her bottom hard enough to leave a handprint.

"Again," she whispers against my lips.

I slap her butt cheeks harder, up to the count of ten before stopping and rubbing her tender flesh. She laughs, and I can't help but join her. "You think that's funny?"

"I think it's kind of sexy."

I pull her into a kiss, showing her how much I care. Harsh and rough, I stroke every crevice, loving her with my tongue. And she submits, moaning while I dominate her mouth. I feel the shift in her as she mewls like a kitten and rubs her nipples against the hair on my chest. I'm hard as a rock again.

"Keep that up and I'm going to be inside you one more time tonight."

"If it pleases you." Her hand slides up my chest to my neck and then to the back of my head. Her fingers glide into my hair, silently encouraging me. "Sir."

****

Kenzie

Slider goes to the bathroom. He returns with a clean belly and a wet wash cloth in his hand. He positions himself between my thighs. He props up on his elbows and gazes at me as he gently washes me.

"I don't think you know how stunning you are. It pisses me off and makes my blood boil every time another man looks at you."

"You make me feel beautiful. I didn't always. I was the girl who was too tall and too thin. The one with the weird-colored hair that wasn't red but wasn't blond either. The one who used a garbage bag as a suitcase."

"You'll never be her again. You're beautiful and mine now." He tosses the washcloth aside, takes my hands, and positions my arms above my head before pulling my knees up, spreading them wide.

He slowly slides inside me until his hips are flush against me. The urge to bury my hands in his hair or grasp his shoulders is strong, but I will not move my arms unless he tells me to. I will prove my submission to him.

We start a slow dance of give-and-take that's so seductive my eyes slowly close. I feel his tongue stroke softly across my extra sensitive nipple, taking it into his mouth and bathing my tender flesh. Then he moves to the other breast and does the same thing. His hands slide under me, lifting me. All this time, he's gliding in and out of my body.

He's making love to me. Tenderly. Carefully. Sincerely. I never want it to end.

"You were made for me. Inside and out was designed with me in mind." His thrusts pick up speed, and he's stroking across the secret spot inside me faster and faster.

"Slider." I say his name over and over.

"Come with me." One hand slides from under me and finds my swollen clit. "Come now."

The wave hits me just as I feel him swell and pulse inside me, filling me. Nothing exists but the two of us. He's completely taken control of my heart.

"Lower your arms."

I open my eyes and follow his instruction.

"Good girl." He holds himself above me for a few seconds while he kisses me tenderly. Then he slides out of me and rolls from the bed.

"I'll be right back."

"I'm not going anywhere."

He returns with another washcloth. He chuckles while gently cleaning me. "We made another mess."

"The alternative is using a condom."

"No way. I like cleaning up my messes." He kisses my stomach, returns to the bathroom, and a moment later slides into bed next to me. He pulls me into his arms and covers us with a sheet. "Rest. Tomorrow, we go back to the real world."

I'm warm and safe and happy and so many other things I don't understand. I fall asleep, knowing I'll be his submissive for as long as he wants me.

****

Moving in with Slider a month ago has turned me into a spoiled woman. He handled everything right down to hiring a company to pack up my apartment and move my things to his place. Sex has only gotten better, and I'm totally used to having multiple orgasms regularly. Yeah. I'm spoiled and loving it.

He has an office at home and is currently moving some of his things to storage so I can have my own space to work when I bring research home with me. He's sequestered this morning, working through a systems issue.

I take a last look in the mirror. My hair is styled, and I'm wearing skinny jeans and a blue sweater. All I need to do is slip on my boots, and I'm ready to go. Kayla and Morgan are picking me up and we're meeting Slider's other partner's wife, Morgan Pierce, at their favorite spa.

I walk down the stairs and tap on Slider's office door. I hear the word "come," and tiny nerve endings tingle. His baritone voice does it every time. I step just inside, not wanting to disturb him if he's on the phone.

His eyes brighten as he stands, walks to meet me, and pulls me flush against his chest. "Enjoy your day with the girls. It's a shame Chelsea couldn't join you, but it might be good that you start with just two of them. From what I've seen and heard, they're both a handful."

"You mean they have minds of their own?" I grin at him.

"Exactly." His serious face slides into place. "Come home in time to rest before we go to Satin. I'm introducing you to the Sybian tonight."

"I promise." I lean in for a kiss, and his arms lock around me. His lips come down hard, his tongue thrusts into my mouth, and he claims me. He's reminding me whom I belong to, and I love it.

My cell dings. It's Kayla and Morgan waiting in the lobby. "I better go."

"Enjoy." He smacks me on my bottom, and I squeal.

I take the elevator down to meet the girls. I'm excited because I've gotten to know them better over the past month. Neither are bashful about performing on the stage occasionally, and I'm totally in awe of them for their bravery.

I'm ushered into the limo and then driven to Morgan's favorite spa. It's one of the most expensive in town, and I'm a little intimidated by the over-the-top luxury. We're greeted by a woman who kisses them both on the cheek and then turns her attention to me.

"Welcome. You are the newest member of the group?"

"I am," I say while leaning down to let her kiss my cheek.

"Such beautiful girls." She turns to Morgan. "We are ready for you in the red salon. Please make yourselves comfortable. Your attendants will take good care of you."

Kayla loops her arm in mine. "Let me tell you about my first trip here."

The rest of the day is a combination of being pampered and me laughing at these two longtime friends. While we move from room to room, they regale me with stories of their lives before and after falling in love with their Doms. Once we've had our massages, facials, private parts waxed, and are sitting in chairs next to each other getting our nails done, I decide to ask a question.

"Did either of you have experience with a Dom or BDSM before you met your husbands?"

Kayla laughs out loud. She has the kind of laugh you join in without knowing what's funny. "Oh, hell no. After Morgan told us about her trip to Club Silken, I threatened to cut off Zack's balls if he hurt her."

Morgan joined the laughter. "She and Chelsea couldn't wait for details. They were knocking on my door the morning after. The first thing Kayla demanded to know was if he had a big dick."

Kayla chokes on a sip of water. She's coughing and laughing at the same time. "I did, didn't I? Inquiring minds needed to know. Besides, we love you and that made the size of his dick important."

I'm so glad to have met these two women. In a short time, I've grown comfortable around them. They're both so gracious, kind, and warm. "You met Nick through Morgan and Zack?"

"Yeah." Kayla leans back in the chair and closes her eyes.

I hope I haven't asked something too personal. I want to have friends. Friends who care about me. Friends who are in it for the long haul. "I'm sorry. I know better than to pry."

Her eyelids pop open, and she smiles. "There's nothing you can't ask or say in front of us. You're one of us now, so expect us to pry, ask embarrassing questions, give you unsolicited advice, and occasionally get you in trouble with Slider."

"What she said." Morgan points a finger at Kayla. "If you have questions or need help navigating your new lifestyle, we're here for you."

I blink back tears of gratitude. "Thank you, both."

Kayla's nails are finished first. She rises and comes to stand next to me. "The first time I walked into Club Silken, Nick took my breath away. I felt this instant connection. He offered to take me on a tour. I wasn't too shocked at the scenes we walked past because of the knowledge I'd gained from Morgan. But Nick and I stopped at a scene where the Dom was using a whip on his sub. Memories from my childhood hit with the strength of a Texas tornado. I freaked and ran from the building."

"She disappeared for six months. I was the one freaking out." Morgan's stunning face was turning red with each word.

Kayla sighs. "I'd also just received word my mom had passed. Morgan's right. I did leave without telling anyone where I'd gone or when I'd be back. Suffice it to say, it wasn't a good time in my life. I turned up just in time to be a part of Morgan's wedding. She and Chelsea welcomed me back with open arms."

I can see the memories of what Kayla went through are still with her. "I'm sorry. I know all about whippings and not having a fun childhood."

I have to try to lighten the conversation. "Nick was still available when you got back?"

A smile lights up her face. "The first time I saw him again was at the wedding. The second I saw Nick in his tuxedo, I knew there was something strong between us."

"You knew going in that he lives the lifestyle?"

"I did. I could write a book with all the research I amassed during the first few weeks of our relationship. He allowed me time to learn and understand."

"Same here." Morgan leans forward to look around Kayla so she can see me. "You have to decide if you enjoy being a sub. I like being the person in charge."

"In charge?" I can't believe she thinks she's in charge of Zack. I've seen them together. She's very subservient to him.

"Everything we do in the bedroom or club is strictly with my permission. I give him my trust, and he, in turn, respects my hard line and never crosses it. At any time, I can stop what we're doing with one word without worrying he'll be upset."

Morgan and I are finished at the same time. The three of us thank everyone who has pampered us and walk out into the parking lot. The limo is idling at the curb as if the driver knew exactly when we'd emerge.

Once we're seated and on the road, I bring up my biggest worry. "I'm defiant and too independent sometimes. It bothers Slider a lot. He thinks I'm not ready or committed to being a sub."

"Outside of the bedroom or the club, Nick and I don't agree all the time. I can't think that you and Slider can't work through it. I've seen the way he looks at you. He's hooked."

"A scene with a whip brought back horrible memories for you, yet you and Nick perform with a cat-o-nine-tails on the stage. How did you work past that?" I hold my breath. Am I getting too personal? "I hard-lined spanking, but Slider regrets agreeing to it more than once."

"I don't believe Slider will ever do anything you don't want." Morgan takes the bottles of water from the small bar and hands one to Kayla and then one to me. "It sounds like he doesn't believe your trust in him is one hundred percent yet. I wish I could help, but you're the only one who can convince him."

The rest of the ride is filled with talk about tonight's get-together at Satin. I haven't met Chelsea and Taylor Horne and am excited to meet them. When Kayla and Morgan learn I haven't bought a new dress for this evening, Morgan makes one call, and we add a stop to our day. I'm an hour late when they drop me off.

I hurry through the lobby, get on the elevator, and key in the code to our floor. I wrap the plastic bag holding my dress over my arm, unlock the door, and go inside.

Slider walks out of his office to greet me. Wearing nothing but low-slung warm-ups, he makes me think sexy thoughts as he walks toward me.

"You're late. I was getting worried."

"I'm sorry. We stopped by the dress shop." I hold the plastic bag behind me. "I don't want you to see it yet."

The blue in his eyes is dark. It's a sure sign I'm in trouble again. "Next time call or text and let me know you're going to be late."

All the happy air my lungs are filled with whooshes out in one long sigh. "I've done something wrong again."

"What?" He opens his arms and I rush to him. Engulfed in his embrace, I rest my head in the crook of his neck. I breathe in his scent, pulling the faint aroma of his cologne deep into my lungs. "No, love. I was a little worried. That's all." He lifts my chin and strokes my jawline with the back of his knuckles. "I care about you. Expect me to be concerned about your well-being."

I open my mouth to speak, but he covers it with his own, scooping me into his arms at the same time. Carrying me upstairs, he deepens the kiss, his tongue demanding cooperation, and I gladly give it.

He gently places my feet on the floor next to the bed. "Take off your clothes and get between the sheets. We still have time for you to rest. I'll take care of dinner."

He takes my new dress and walks to the closet to hang it up. My heart is racing while I strip as fast as I can, leaving my garments on the floor in a pile. I have a surprise for him and don't want him to see it until tonight. I jump under the covers and put them up to my neck.

Slider sits on the edge of the bed. "If I told you all the dirty things I want to do to you right now, you'd dress and run."

"Never." I shake my head. "You're stuck with me."

"Same." He stands, leans down, and kisses my forehead.

I don't tell him how wet he's made me just by talking about his desires. "That makes me happy."

"Get some rest. I'll wake you in an hour."

Chapter 13

Slider

I lean against the doorway and watch her sleep. She's on her side, knees bent, hands curled under her chin, and her beautiful hair is spread across the pillow. The sheet has slipped just far enough for the tops of her delicate breasts to be on display. I hate to wake her, so I remain motionless, enjoying the scene in front of me for a minute.

My chest tightens. With each heartbeat, the word *mine* seems to get louder. She's become such a vital part of my life so quickly. I can't imagine life without her.

Kenzie rolls onto her back. The sheet slides down to her waist, and her eyelids flutter open. A soft smile graces her face when her hand slides under the covers. I'm mesmerized and stare as she moves it lower and lower.

"Are you going to stand there and watch or join me?"

My dick presses against my slacks, begging to be released. *Do I let her get away with trying to control what happens in our bedroom this one time?*

"Please, sir." She removes her hand and holds up a finger.

I can see she's wet from here. "Lick those juices off your finger."

She obeys, her tongue lapping at that nectar that will soon be mine. "I think I taste strawberries."

I laugh hard. "I'll be the judge of that."

"Looks like we're going to be late." She opens her arms wide.

I cross the room in three steps before stripping the sheet off her. I kick off my shoes, shuck my clothes, and crawl between her legs. There's no foreplay, I spread her wide, and slide into her wet pussy. I'm home. I'm where I belong.

****

I'm hard as steel and have been since Kenzie walked down the stairs at the apartment. She's wearing a corset that barely contains her breasts. Skin-colored fabric is see-through and stretched tight around her perfect body. The skirt starts at her hips and just covers the bottom curve of her ass. Thank fuck diamond-shaped patches of leather are strategically placed to cover her pussy and nipples.

The drive to Satin has been torture. I've kept my hands off her, knowing she's excited about tonight. If I were a nicer person, I'd have given her a couple of orgasms to tide her over, but I want her on the edge. I park, get out, and go open her door. I assist Kenzie out of my car, wrap my hands in the fur surrounding her, and pull her close. "I can't stop staring at you. I'm going to have to kill every male in the club for looking at what's mine."

"They can't see that part of me."

"It's a damn good thing." I reach inside my coat pocket and pull out a long thin box. "Before we go in." I open it, revealing the four-row diamond choker.

Her hand slaps my chest and tears fill her eyes. "Oh my God. It's beautiful."

"You're beautiful."

She turns her back to me and lifts her hair. I slide the necklace into place but pause. "You understand I'm putting a collar on you. It's not just a piece of jewelry. Everyone inside will understand that you belong to me."

"I'll shout it from the rooftop if you like."

I fasten the choker and her fingers lift to trace the stones. She whispers something I don't understand. "What was that?"

"Nothing." She moves next to me and slips her hand through my arm. "I'm looking forward to tonight."

I think I know what she said. I hope I'm right. We climb the steps and enter the foyer. I'm surprised to see Gabriel at the desk. He's running the safety department for all four clubs. He must be filling in for one of his employees. He stands and reaches for a wristband. His expression changes when he sees the necklace. He glances at me with approval shining in his eyes. I'm glad he likes her. He's become a big part of our little pieced-together family.

"Good evening." He smiles at Kenzie and nods at me. "May I take your coat?"

"Hello, Gabriel." She slides her faux fur off her shoulders and passes it to him. His eyes widen. It's fleeting and almost unnoticeable, but his appreciation of her beauty is there.

"How's it going?" The parking lot is almost full and I'm pleased he's on-site.

"Everyone inside seems to be having a good time. I started to call you with the news about Rachel but knew you'd be here tonight."

"News?" I ask.

"I've been keeping up with the case. Her father negotiated a deal for her. She's going to a mental rehab center in California for a year." Gabriel's scowl says he doesn't approve.

"A plush resort, no doubt," Kenzie grumbles.

I squeeze her hand. "She's gone. Let's not let it ruin our night."

She looks up with excitement written all over her face. "You're right. Fuck her."

"No, thanks," Gabriel and I say at the same time.

The three of us laugh as Gabriel opens the main door into the club for us. "Enjoy."

I open the inside door to the club, and slow, sensual music greets us. My hand rests on her lower back while we walk to the far side of the club where our friends are waiting. Kayla is the first to see us.

"Oh. My. God. The building is going to catch fire," Kayla announces to our friends, Nick, Morgan, Zack, Chelsea, and Taylor sitting at the table.

"What?" Nick's head turns in the direction Kayla is looking. His lips curl into a smile as his eyes travel down and back up Kenzie's body.

A swirl of jealousy followed by pure masculine pride fills my chest. I glance at Kenzie and sense her nerves. "Ignore the stares."

"Yes, Sir." She lowers her head but not before I see her smile.

At that moment, I know there's nothing I won't do to make her happy. "While we're here, out front, it's acceptable to keep your head up. For now, we're just hanging out with friends."

"But if I do that when we go to the room?" Her eyes sparkle with mischief.

"You'll get that spanking you asked for a while back."

I feel eyes watching us as we join our friends. I get her seated and then sit back. "Ladies. Did you enjoy your day at the spa?"

Kayla perks up. "We had a blast. Thank you."

"My pleasure. Who do I thank for steering Kenzie to the dress shop?"

"Me," Morgan and Kayla say at the same time.

"She looks stunning." Kayla's eyebrows lift. "Doesn't she?"

"Absolutely. But then I think she's stunning with no clothes on."

"Oh, hell, yes," Nick says, quickly pulling Kayla in for a hug. "Of course, I'm referring to my wife."

We order drinks and listen to the ladies talk for a while. I check my watch at the same time my club manager walks up to the table.

"We're about fifteen minutes from the demonstration. The good seats will fill fast."

Zack stands, offering his hand to Morgan. "I think we'd better get going."

"Zack and I are the entertainment tonight. You missed our last performance. Come watch," Morgan explains to Kenzie.

She looks at me with a question in her eyes.

I lean over and whisper in her ear. "Not this time. I have plans for you."

She shivers. "Good."

"Are you cold?" I think I know the answer, but I ask anyway.

"No. Just thinking about what's coming."

"Come with me and I'll show you."

Our friends move to the seating area in front of the stage while I lead Kenzie to the back of the club to our private room. I pause outside the door to remind her everything changes when we step inside.

Before I can speak, I see her gaze pointed at her feet and her hands are clasped behind her back. I've never asked for this position, but I understand it's her way of submitting. I open the door and let her walk inside. I seal us away from the outside world.

We're in the largest playroom of the club. It's used only by elite members or owners. She stops and runs her fingers over the straps on the swing before checking out the padded leather cuffs on the suspension bar, the breeding stand with cuffs to hold her legs suspended, a bondage yoke, and the spanking bench. Lastly, she stops and walks a circle around the massive bed in the corner. Her eyes are wide when she turns. Her gaze drops to the floor.

"Interesting stuff, Sir."

"You missed a couple of things."

"I don't want to get in the cage."

I cross the room to her. "I will never put you in one of those. They're used for humiliation, and I will never do that to you." I pull her face to mine, wrap my arms around her, and kiss her with everything I have. I'm not sure how much longer I could have watched her peruse the equipment. "You'll ride the Sybian tonight."

My hands find the lace ties that hold her corset on her body. My urge is to rip it off of her, but I hold myself back. "Undress and put your clothes on the counter by the door."

Her eyes lift but her head remains lowered. "Yes, Sir."

"I need to see your eyes while we're in here. Look at me."

Her gaze is filled with pure lust. She's excited by the things she's seen. I step back and let her strip. She's barefooted as she walks to the front of the room and carefully places her outfit exactly as instructed. Turning, waiting for more instructions, she looks like a goddess. Her full breasts, flat stomach, and long athletic legs make my cock press hard against the restraint of my slacks.

"Let's try out the swing. It's suspended from the ceiling and completely safe." I walk her to it, letting her look at and handle the wide straps. The next time we come to this room, I'll expect obedience, but she's still learning, so I step back and give her a minute. "The back brace and saddle help keep you in place. The stirrups position your thighs and legs just right."

She studies the swing for a second. She looks over her shoulder at me. Her eyes shine with lust. "Hmm. Makes for easy access."

"For me, yes. You just enjoy." I pull her into my arms and crush my mouth onto hers. Her warm naked flesh under my hands has me so hard it's almost painful. That she's eager to try anything I ask of her heats my blood.

A few minutes later, I have her suspended with her legs spread wide. Her bare pussy is spread open and sopping wet. Her cheeks are pink as she looks at the straps secured right above her knees.

"This feels weird."

"Are you uncomfortable?"

"No. Just don't leave me alone."

"Never." I press the lift button and raise her a little higher. "This is a buffet at eye level."

I lean closer to her and inhale the scent of her arousal. Her chest is rising and falling rapidly. I can't wait any longer. I feel like the hummingbird with his first scent of nectar. I lean over and lick my gorgeous woman from her ass hole to her mound. Her gasp makes me smile.

"Oh. My God." She tries to help me, struggles to lift her hips.

I smack her bare butt. "I'm in control here. Relax and enjoy."

Her head falls back, and I take my time teasing her. My tongue runs around her swollen outer lips and circles her opening again and again. I place an open mouth on her pussy and mimic what I will do to her soon but with my cock. Her body trembles but I continue my assault, making her wait.

"Slider. I need more. Please, Sir." She stretches out the word *sir* for a long couple of seconds.

"What do you need? Tell me."

"Oh. My God. Suck my clit. Please."

"Since you said please." I latch onto her and lash her with the tip of my tongue before pulling the tiny nub into my mouth and doing as she asked. I slide two fingers inside her and pump them in and out.

I recognize the warning signs and bring her to the edge of an orgasm but pull off. I cup her breasts, squeezing the soft flesh, kneading, and pinching her nipples until the crisis is over. I lift my head and kiss the top of her mound.

"I'm dying. Please let me come, Sir."

"No." I walk away and undress, returning with a vibrating wand. "This is a Thunder Stick. Let's see if you like it." I turn it on and press it against her clit.

"I can't stop it," she cries out.

"Yes, you can." I turn off the wand, lower her, and then slide my cock deep into her hot, needy pussy. I hold still and relish the contractions going on inside her. "You won't come until I say you can."

"Yes." The sound is more of a sigh of relief that I've filled her instead of an agreement.

I grasp her hips, pull out, and punch back in hard, starting a rhythm that increases until she's begging, and I'm on the verge of emptying myself in her heat.

"So good. So good." The sounds of flesh on flesh and her guttural moans fill the air. I could listen to the sounds she makes forever.

"Come now. I need to feel your cum soaking my cock."

Her eyes close and her body jerks. Her pussy tightens around me as if trying to prevent me from sliding out. Her spasms and nonsensical words are too much, and I drive home one last time, and while holding her hips tight against me, I release streams of cum inside her.

I quickly release her, gather her in my arms, and sit on the couch. I pull the lightweight blanket over her and wait for her to recover.

Kenzie lifts her head and kisses me. It's a soft, closed-mouth number that would have made my knees weak if I'd been standing.

"Let me get us some water."

She crawls off me and wraps herself back up. "I'd like that."

I stop and watch her for a minute as she stares off in the distance. I have to wonder where her mind is and what she's thinking. I sit next to her, open her bottle, and hand it to her. "You need to rest before you take on the Sybian."

"Yes, Sir." I realize her eyes are focused on the machine. "How does it work?"

"You straddle it."

"Like riding a horse?"

"Yeah."

She snuggles against me. Her fingers draw lines through the hair on my chest. I inhale when she pinches my nipple.

"Does that feel good?"

"Oh, yes. Anytime you touch my body, I like it."

We finish our water, and she scoots to the edge of the couch. "Show me how it works."

My heart rate kicks up. "I love how enthusiastic you are to try new things."

"I wouldn't be this fascinated without you."

I stab my hand into her hair and drag her to me. My lips cover hers, my tongue breaches her mouth, and I sweep inside her. Claim her. We're both breathing hard when I end the kiss. I extend my hand and help her stand.

"This way, love."

She stands to the side while I set up the Sybian with one silicone bulb-shaped stimulator protruding from the front hole. Dropping a little lube over it, I slide my hand up and down coating it for her. She laughs while she watches.

"What's funny?"

She points at my hand. "You masturbating that thing."

I step back and smile at her. "Get your ass over here."

"Yes, Sir."

I can't keep the smile from my face. She approaches everything with a wide-open mind and excitement. "Swing your leg over and position your pussy above your new lover."

She blinks and looks up at me. "You're the only lover I want."

"That's good because mine's the last real dick you'll ever have inside your body again." I clamp my mouth shut. I've said too much.

Her height gives her a distinct advantage when it comes to mounting this behemoth. She swings her leg over and pauses, hovering instead of seating herself. Her eyebrows lift. She's waiting for me to give her permission.

"That G-Egg attachment is designed to stimulate your G-spot. Slowly lower yourself onto it." I hold her hand to steady her as she eases herself down.

"How's that feel?"

"Weird. Not uncomfortable.

I drag a chair closer so I can sit in front of her and the Sybian. Her hand lowers between her legs. She locates the large egg and aligns her body with it. Then she slowly descends while my cock protests loudly by pushing against my zipper.

"There are many sizes and shapes we can choose from." I attach a red riser that raises the attachment against her clit.

"Oh," she grins and leans forward.

"I should warn you it's loud. We had a rubber mat put under it to muffle the sound." I reach in my pocket and pull out the remote control. I press the button to the lowest setting.

"Oh!" Kenzie jumps as the egg starts to move. "Oh. My God."

My dick throbs as I tell her to come when she wants. While I'm tempted to slide my dick into her mouth, I don't. This isn't about me. I want her to know my world intimately. All aspects. I change the speed to the third level.

The noisy machine must not disturb her because her head falls back and her hair swings side to side. Before we ordered the Sybian we read that orgasms come quickly with the G-Egg, and the look on Kenzie's face confirms it. I increase the intensity once more and her mouth falls open.

I almost come like some horny teenager watching his first porn movie. Her moans fill the room and her body convulses. I give her time to settle down and when the afterglow sets in, I turn off the machine.

"Come here, love." I pull her into my arms, carry her to the bed, and gently place her against a stack of pillows. Her hands grip my arms, pulling me down to her.

"Hold me." The corners of her lips lift. "Sir."

I roll her to face me and love how she throws a leg over my hip. She rolls her shoulders and I revel in the sated look in her eyes. "Next time we'll use two dildos."

"I barely survived one." Her fingers caress my cheek. "It was interesting, but nothing compares to having you inside me."

****

Kenzie

I see not only lust but affection in Slider's eyes. He keeps referring to me as "love," and my heart is hoping he's being literal. I just need him to say it out loud.

I start to run my hands down his arms but stop. "May I touch you?"

His eyes turn even darker. "I'd like that."

I slide my hands through the hair on his chest and over his nipples. The curls taper to a thin line that leads me to his erection. I bypass it and move down the bed to his bare feet. I rub his instep with my thumbs. His groan spurs me on and I apply pressure for a few minutes. I slide my hands up his legs to his crotch and cup his balls. I love the feel of him in my hand. I lower my head and his cock stands up as if to meet me. I kiss the head and roll my tongue around him. I raise my eyes and find him staring at me.

"You're so beautiful." He pushes himself against the headboard. "Come here."

"As you wish."

I crawl between his legs until his hand grasps his erection and the other the back of my head. "Open your mouth and suck me."

I lap at the pre-cum oozing from the tip before sliding my tongue over him. I take him to the back of my throat and suck my way back to the top.

"Fuck." A primal growl rolls from him. He wraps my hair around his hand and his hips pump toward my mouth.

I have no control over what's happening. He's fucking my mouth and I gladly surrender. Each time he pulls back, I run my tongue around the head of his cock and then down the silky underside of him. He bounces against the back of my throat. I relax and take even more of him deep. My saliva coats him and drips from the corners of my mouth. His groans send moisture sliding down the inside of my thighs.

My pussy throbs, begging for his attention. I look up and see him watching me. He tries to pull out of my mouth, but I shake him off. I pull back, find the small slit on the head and press the tip of my tongue against it, and then sink until my nose touches his pubic hair.

"Fuck. Stop or I'm going to explode." His hands, buried in my hair, tug me off him. "Turn over onto your hands and knees."

It's not a request but a command, one I happily obey. I scramble into position. Head down and ass up. My body is aching for him. "Please. I need you."

He enters me with one hard thrust. He's so deep I feel him against my cervix. He leans forward, bracing himself with his arms, and bites and licks my back and shoulders. His movement is slow at first, as if savoring every moment, but soon it escalates. His hands grip my hips and he pistons inside me.

"I need to come," I plead.

His thumb rubs in my juices and slides back to circle my butt hole. A little pressure and he breaches me. His movements match his thrusts.

"Please," I beg again. Lightning races through my bloodstream. It's circling, threatening, warning.

"Come for me, love. Now."

My toes curl, my mind blanks, and my body writhes beneath him. He groans, and I feel him come. Strong jets of his seed pulse from him, sending a second orgasm barreling through me. I try not to collapse as my body twitches while I clench and pulse around him. Then my knees give out.

We land facedown. Neither of us speaks. I can tell I'm not holding his full weight but right now it doesn't matter. We just exist for a few minutes. He slowly slips from my body and rolls onto his side, turning me onto my back.

"You okay?" He smooths my damp hair away from my face. His eyes are soft and there's no tension in his face. He looks euphoric. My heart swells.

I smile at his question. "I'm better than okay."

"Yes, you are." His knuckles stroke my cheek. He does that often and I love it. "You're perfect."

I chuckle. "That's post-coital bliss."

"No. It's love. I love you."

I blink rapidly, trying to stem the flow of tears. It doesn't work.

"Wait. Hey. I'll take it back if it makes you unhappy."

"Don't you dare." I playfully punch him in the chest.

"I don't know what to do with a crying woman. Much less when it's my woman."

"Oh, Slider. I love you so much."

"Thank God." He brushes my cheeks dry with his thumbs and then pulls me onto his chest. "You mean everything to me. I promise to move heaven and earth to show you just how much I love you."

We lie in silence for a few minutes. Both of us probably feeling the ramifications of genuinely loving another person. I swear my heart swells in my chest. He loves me.

"Slider?"

I feel a kiss on the top of my head. "Hmm?"

"No one's ever said I love you to me."

His arms tighten around me. "Get used to it. You'll be hearing it a lot from now on."

I like that he doesn't rationalize my pain away. He accepts it and assures me there's more love coming. "That makes me very happy."

"Let's go home."

I look into his eyes. "Yes, Sir."

Epilogue

Kenzie

Six months later

I turn my face to the sun, and a dark shadow blocks my view. I lift my sunglasses and smile at the hunk holding my drink.

"You ordered a sex on the beach?" He hands the cold glass to me.

"I never 'order' anything. I'm married to a Dom, and he wouldn't approve." I put the straw in my mouth and suck, loving the groan coming from him.

Slider walks around me and stretches out in the chaise next to mine. His long hard body has tanned over the past three weeks while we island-hopped from Curaçao to Barbados to our last stop, Saint-Barthélemy Island. It's been the most wonderful honeymoon a girl could have. There's been no outside phone calls, no place one of us has to be, and no set time to get up in the morning. I whisper a cuss word at the thought of getting back into a routine.

"I heard that and agree."

"What are you agreeing to?" I get up and go stand by his chair.

"Hating to go home tomorrow." He slides over and I squeeze onto the lounger with him.

"I still can't believe my boss let me have time off. I haven't worked there for a full year yet."

"I may have given your boss's boss a huge price break on a new system we just put on the market."

"You didn't." I punch his tight abs.

"I did. Your firm uses our operating system anyway. I just offered him an upgrade. He and I both got one." Slider's hand cups my bare breast. "I also chose only islands where topless sunbathing is allowed."

I slide my hand under the waistband of his swim trunks and rake the tips of my fingernails from the base of his cock to the head. He instantly starts to harden. "I love causing that reaction in you."

"Never fails. Nudity is against the law. Maybe we should go to our suite and finish this because I'm going to strip you naked and be inside you soon."

I remove my hand, push off his chest, and then stand. I lean over, letting my breasts dangle close to his lips. I whisper, "This is our last night here. I'm not hungry. Let's cancel our dinner reservation."

The sly grin on his face tells me I said exactly the right thing. Excitement races through me and I shiver.

"Works for me." He lifts his head far enough to slide his tongue across my nipple. I already have what I'm going to eat."

SKYWAY to HELL
A new Lost and Found, Inc. Romantic Suspense
Unedited

Prologue

The sound of ice cubes swirling around an otherwise empty glass accentuated the customer's impatience. He'd finished his third drink in record time.

Her coworker turned away from him and whispered, "That jerk makes my skin crawl. He tried to run his hand under my skirt."

"Oh really? I'll go this time."

"I'm not going to argue."

As she approached him, his gaze dropped to her feet and traveled no further up than her breasts. She crowded close to him. "Your impatience tells me you'd like another drink."

"I'm always thirsty, sweetheart." He shifted, taking advantage of her nearness, lowered his arm, and ran his fingers across the back of her knee. "A man like me has a big appetite."

She smiled down at him. "And how does a man 'like' you satisfy his appetite?"

"With a tasty meal." His hand slid up to her thigh. "Like you."

"You're in the mood for a special kind of pleasure tonight, aren't you?" She'd spoken softly so he alone could hear her words.

"Always." His gaze finally lifted to her face and his lips pulled back showing icy white veneers. "My God, you are a Madonna."

"I don't think that's quite accurate." She caught his gaze with hers. "A Madonna is a virtuous woman"

"Honey, I don't need a virtuous woman tonight."

She placed her hand on his knee and squeezed. "Do you have a place in mind?"

"How about the Milenium?"

She pretended to be considering his offer. "Excellent choice. Mister…" She paused, testing him.

"Sumptner. Donald to you."

"Well, Donald, leave an envelope at the desk with your room card key inside."

"Who should I say is picking up the envelope?" His hand inched up her leg.

Memories of dark rooms, filthy hands, and sweaty bodies flashed through her mind.

"Madonna."

Chapter 1

Dalton Murphy pushed away from his desk and walked down the hall to the boss's office. Nate Wolfe and the rest of the Lost and Found team had made him comfortable from the day he joined the team. The company was growing so fast Dalton had already lost his ranking of the newest member. This group of former military men not only took on government jobs but a lot of their work was done helping people who had nowhere to turn and needed help. He hadn't once regretted leaving the FBI to be part of this organization.

Nate, standing in front of his desk, waved Dalton inside. "Come in. Mrs. Vardon requested to speak with the both of us."

She extended her hand. "Yes. That's true."

Dalton held his surprise in check, pushed his hatred for the woman's husband aside, and took her hand. He'd been in charge of the unit assigned to bring down her husband, Vincent Vardon, to justice. Being reminded of failure soured in Dalton's stomach. "Mrs. Vardon."

"Call me Marcy."

Nate, who never missed even the slightest reaction in people, backed up and perched on edge of his desk. "Is there a problem?"

"I investigated her husband while I was with the FBI."

"That's in the past and not a problem for me." Mrs. Vardon's fingers tugged at the hem of her shirt. "Dalton knows Vincent's history."

"Why don't you tell us how we can help?" Dalton sat in the chair next to her. Had fate presented him with a chance to make another run at her husband?

She pulled a picture from her handbag and handed it to him. "I want you to bring my husband's body home. I want it done quickly and quietly. The media will be salivating if this situation gets out."

Dalton studied the picture. Vardon's arms and legs were spread-eagle on a bed. His eyes were half-closed as if he were admiring his dick which was standing at attention.

"There's a message on the back." Mrs. Vardon slid forward to the edge of her chair.

Dalton turned over the picture and read aloud, "You'll find his body at the Millennium in Monterrey, Mexico under the name Donald Sumptner."

"Too bad it's not signed." Dalton passed the picture to Nate.

"Vincent never had an erection like that with me." Vardon's wife crossed her legs, her skirt slid higher up her thighs. "Somebody slipped him more than one blue pill."

"Why was your husband in Mexico?" Nate put the snapshot on his desk. "He doesn't look dead to me. Other than the comment, what makes you think he's dead?"

"He said he had business to take care of." Mrs. Vardon huffed out a pfft sound. "My attorney has been in contact with the Mexican government. They have his body but refuse to release it until an autopsy had been performed."

Nate returned to his chair behind the desk and looked at Dalton. "You want this case?"

Mrs. Vardon rubbed her eyes, leaving a smudge of mascara under both. "If you won't

help me, I'll find someone who will."

Vincent Vardon was responsible for the murders of a witness and one of the agents who'd guarded her. This might be a chance to dig into his business and make things right. "Yeah. I'll make a run to Mexico. See what I can learn."

Mrs. Vardon opened her purse, removed her wallet, and wrote a check without asking for an amount. "Will this cover a retainer?"

Nate accepted it with a nod. "We'll start right away."

Dalton also stood, shook her hand, and escorted her to the door. He watched her drive away, turned, and found Nate leaning against the door jamb of his office watching.

"Interesting woman," Nate said. "You have a dog in this hunt?"

"I do." Dalton smiled at Nate's colorful description. "A lot of people died because of Vardon's gun-running. I'd like to close the business down."

"Do it." Nate slapped Dalton on his back and walked to his desk. "If you need us, we're here for you."

Dalton returned to his office, closed the door, and called his old boss, learning an agent was already in Mexico and would be his contact.

His mind was racing as he booked his trip to Monterrey. When he looked up, Marcus Ricci and his dog, Diablo, were watching through the glass wall. Dalton waved them inside.

Marcus sat and the dog dropped next to his master's feet, resting one paw on top of Marcus's boot. "What are you and Nate cooking up?"

Dalton brought Marcus up to speed.

"Ah, the one who got away?"

"The one I wanted in the worst way."

"Where you headed?"

"Monterrey, Mexico."

"Lucky bastard." Marcus shook his head. "Try to have some fun while you're there. You could use it."

"What does that mean? I have fun."

"Doing what?"

Dalton stiffened in his chair.

Marcus stood and so did Diablo. "We're here if you need us."

Dalton nodded his head in understanding. "So I've heard."

****

Ashley Hunter studied the picture on her computer screen to gain insight into the man she would work with here in Mexico. There wasn't much to learn since most of his assignments while with the agency had been redacted.

His photo was the typical black and white FBI shot where you're told to look at the camera and don't blink. Dalton Murphy had a rugged, masculine, with a take no prisoners face. His gorgeous dark eyes looked as if they held dark secrets. Secrets that had been redacted. Even with no hint of a smile, his mouth appeared to be soft and kissable. "So why did you walk away?" she mumbled to no one.

"You could just ask me." The male voice coming from behind her had a cold edge.

Ashley closed the page, rolled back her chair, and turned to find Dalton Murphy leaning against a column. He walked toward her, his movements were fluid and predatory. His gaze locked with hers and those kissable lips slid into a scowl.

If he'd wanted to frighten her, he'd failed.

"Ashley Hunter." She smiled and extended her hand, which was immediately swallowed with his firm grip. "I wasn't expecting you until this afternoon."

"Obviously." Dalton released her and looked over her shoulder at her blank computer screen. "Any gaps I can fill in for you?"

"I was curious about the legendary Dalton Murphy." Ignoring his question, she sat and pointed to the chair next to the desk she'd been temporarily assigned. "You must have been having a bad day when they took your ID picture."

"What have you learned about the victim?" Dalton remained standing.

Okay, so maybe he was a tad intimidating. Hell, his size would jumble anybody's nerves.

"I know the body has been identified as Vincent Vardon. He's an American citizen who has been under investigation more than once." She paused. "Why are you interested in this case?"

Dalton lowered himself to the chair, his thigh muscles straining against his jeans. He'd rolled up the sleeves on his shirt revealing tan skin and muscular arms. She wanted to ask him about the redacted pieces of information in his file, but her curiosity was squashed by irritation flashing behind his eyes.

He opened his mouth but then closed it. For a few long seconds, he studied her face as if planning his words carefully. "You do understand that we're on two separate missions? You need to verify if a playing card was found with Vardon's body, and if so, was it the Queen of Hearts. I've been hired to ensure his body goes home posthaste."

"Anyone could have 'ensured' the body made it home. And how do you know about the card? You know too much about the murder to be just an escort. Why you? Vardon's dead."

Dalton's expression remained unchanged. "I like the bastard dead but preferred him alive and in my hands."

"You don't play well with others, do you?" Not expecting an answer, Ashley handed Dalton the few documents that she'd managed to pull together.

"I don't play."

She tried to breathe through her frustration while he thumbed through the paperwork. Her temporary partner cocked his head to the side.

"This is all you have?"

"I haven't been here but a few hours. So far, I know what airlines Vardon flew to Mexico on, what time the plane landed, and which credit card he used for the taxi ride to the Millennium Hotel."

"But he didn't register at the hotel under his name."

"I don't know that. The hotel manager refused to confirm or deny anything." Damn, she'd sounded like she was making excuses but it was the truth.

"I assure you Vardon used an alias." Dalton unzipped the outside pocket on his suitcase, removed a picture, and passed it to her. "Mrs. Vardon received this earlier today."

Ashley stared at a naked man with a rock-hard erection. Tilting the photo into different angles, she hummed. If he thought she'd be shocked, he was wrong. "That's impressive."

"Read the message on the back." He huffed out what sounded like a chuckle.

She turned over the picture, read the note, and then passed it back to Dalton. "He used Donald Sumptner as his alias. That explains the confusion in getting the body identified."

"Vardon's wife wants as few leaks to the press as possible." Dalton returned the picture to his suitcase.

"Good luck with that."

"Who found him?" Dalton's short sentences didn't give her any encouragement that he was going to be helpful. He was holding out on her. She'd read enough about him to know he didn't take jobs to escort a criminal's body home for the hell of it.

"Hotel housekeeping."

"Any news on the autopsy?"

"It was scheduled for late yesterday."

"We need those results."

"I agree." Ashley suppressed the urge to say 'duh'. "First, I'd appreciate you telling me the real reason you're here."

The dark stubble on Dalton's face didn't hide the tiny indentation in Dalton's chin, nor did it conceal the twitch in his jaw. It was as if he was deciding what or how much to tell her.

"To heal a scab I've been picking at for three years."

"Well, that was helpful." She rolled her eyes. "Are you referring to Vardon's acquittal?"

"Do you ever give up?"

"No."

"I guessed as much."

Ashley distinctly heard him growl before he dropped her folder on the desk.

"I know somebody who might help. I haven't spoken with him in years, but if he's still working, I'll ask." Dalton pulled his cell from his pocket, scrolled through contacts, and then tapped a number. He put his cell on speaker and held it between them.

"Nunez." The voice on the line was smooth but without a hint of welcome.

"I'll be damn, I wasn't sure you'd still be alive." Dalton's tone had warmed and a hint of a smile lifted the corners of his mouth.

She bit back the urge to get too hopeful. She'd been tasked with determining if this death tied back to three other murders in the states. With Dalton's help, she might turn this trip into more than a quick assignment and be recognized as an agent who could handle any case that came her way. To date, she was still proving herself.

"I'm more surprised that you are, old friend. How can I help the FBI?" The change in Dalton's tone of voice on the phone was immediate and warm.

"I'm no longer with the agency, but I am working a case with them. I'm also in Monterrey."

"That sounds like a long story, but I'm guessing you don't have time to tell me."

"Tonight, over dinner?"

"If you're buying. There's a steak house named El Choro. Meet me there at eight."

"Sounds good."

"Now, tell me why you have crossed the border into my country."

"You heard about Vincent Vardon's murder?"

"Who hasn't? His wife's attorney has contacted anyone who'll listen. She gave us the alias he used. I figured you'd be pleased the bastard was dead."

"My only regret is that I didn't kill him." The nerves in Dalton's jaw started twitching again. "I need your help getting information about his murder."

"The FBI is supposed to be here looking into it."

"The FBI is here." Ashley leaned closer to the cell phone. "The autopsy was scheduled for last night. Can you get the results?"

"Dalton." Detective Nunez made a tsk-tsk-tsk sound. "This person's voice is much more pleasing than yours."

"Sorry," Dalton said. "I should have introduced you."

"Special Agent Ashley Hunter," she spoke up.

"Detective Rodrigo Nunez. For you, senora, I'll see what I can do." If a person could flirt with words, he was, and she liked him sight unseen.

"It's senorita and I appreciate your help."

"No problem. Be wary, senorita. Dalton has a way with the ladies."

"Shit up, Rod," Dalton said. "We'd also appreciate a look inside Vardon's hotel room."

"You ask a lot, my friend."

"I know." Dalton's tone of voice was relaxed with the detective. "The quicker we get answers the quicker we get out of your hair."

"Meet me at the morgue in two hours."

"Thank you," she said.

"Don't thank me yet." Nunez ended the call.

"So even though you're not assigned to investigate this case, you're looking into it." That Dalton had included her when requesting access to the hotel room earned him serious points.

"I'm a curious guy." Dalton stood and glanced at his watch. "Let's get me checked in so I can ditch this bag and then we can stop somewhere to eat on the way to the morgue." His forehead wrinkled as his dark eyes raked across her face. His gaze seemed to map every inch.

"You're staring."

"You're observant." He continued to study her. "I thought you looked familiar, but it didn't register until you introduced yourself to Rod. Is it possible you're related to a Houston Detective named Ash Hunter?"

"Ashton? You know my brother?"

Dalton nodded. "And the world gets smaller." One corner of his mouth curved upward. It wasn't exactly a smile but it was enough to set her heart pounding. "I've only met him once, but we've spoken over the phone a couple of times." He gestured toward the door. "You ready?"

"Absolutely." She slipped her cell into her pocket and headed out of the building. Tonight, she'd call her brother and learn more about Dalton.

****

Dalton let Special Agent Ashley Hunter take the lead and followed her across the parking lot. She moved like a woman who knew exactly where she was and where she was going. Her blonde hair, the color of wheat just before harvest, pulled back in a low ponytail, glistened under the sun's rays. High cheekbones and piercing blue eyes complimented her creamy skin. None of those things had caught his attention as much as her mouth. Her lips, lush and plump, had sent a surge of blood straight to his dick, kicking his imagination into gear with all the uses he could find for them.

The typical FBI kakis slacks, white blouse, and navy jacket helped camouflage her figure but didn't keep him from noticing the way her hips swayed as she walked. His immediate reaction to her was uncharacteristic and he didn't like it one damn bit. Dalton shook the X-rated thoughts from his mind and tried to concentrate on their surroundings.

This part of Monterrey reflected a recovering economy with modern buildings and streets that had been well maintained. The crime rate was probably lower in this area as opposed to other parts of town. Too bad life had gotten better for some but not for all.

Dalton had been here a few times with Rodrigo when they'd been on military leave. Even in the poor neighborhoods where drugs, theft, and murder were rampant, most of the people had been warm and friendly. The young men and girls living in that area had few choices. They could go it alone or join a gang. Not much of an option for a kid.

The wheels of change turned slowly, but with cops like Rod Nunez on the job, progress would happen.

"I'm parked right here." Dalton stopped at the back of his rental. "I'll drive if you like."

"Works for me. I'll navigate. Where are you staying?" she asked as they both got in the car.

"At the Milenium."

"Isn't that convenient? That's where Vardon was registered." She slipped off the jacket. "Man, it's hot."

"Leave the jacket in the car. I won't tell on you if you break regulations." The second he got into the car Dalton turned the air to the max.

"You know my boss." She placed her coat in the back seat and joined him in the car. "It was one of the things in your file that wasn't redacted."

"I don't lie. I don't care if you wear a T-shirt and jeans. It's nobody's business but yours."

"Turn right at the next stop sign. There's a locally owned restaurant in the middle of the block. Your accent tells me you're a native Texas boy so I think you'll like the food."

Dalton made the turn as directed. He parked in front of the small café, got out, and waited for Ashley. Strips of paint had peeled off the sign so badly he couldn't decipher the name of the place.

"Is this okay?" She opened the door to the restaurant for him.

"Thank you, ma'am." He nodded as he walked past her. "Absolutely. The best food usually comes from local cooks."

They walked inside and following instructions seated themselves. The colorful walls and decorations, the strong aromas drifting from the kitchen, reminded him of a long time ago when life was fun.

Chips and salsa arrived with the waitress and they ordered their lunch.

"So," Ashley picked up a chip and pointed it at him. "We work side-by-side gathering and sharing information?"

He understood the lack of trust flashing in her eyes. "Sure."

"Good."

Dalton dipped a chip into the salsa. "It wouldn't surprise me if this was a weapons deal gone bad."

"Oh, I don't think so. This was personal. He really pissed somebody off."

"What makes you think that?" Dalton filled his mouth with the loaded chip.

"Rumor has it Vardon's penis was cut off and stuffed in his mouth."

She had perfect timing because his surprise at her comment and the blinding heat of the peppers hit his taste buds arrived at the same time. As a native-born Texan, no way was Dalton admitting the salsa had burned off the top layer of his tongue. He swallowed a cough and casually lifted his water glass to his lips and drank.

"Water just intensifies the burn." She grabbed a tortilla, slathered it with butter, and then handed it to him.

He ate the tortilla then took a second sip of water. The woman either had a great sense of humor or was pure evil. Judging by the sparkle in her eyes and the smile on her face, he could guess which. She was enjoying his pain.

"Premortem or postmortem?"

She lifted one shoulder. "I don't know if the rumor is true or not."

Their food arrived and both fell silent. Dalton concentrated on his beef enchiladas, rice, and refried beans and Ashley ate her chicken fajitas.

The waitress returned with the check and laid it on the table, staying to chat with Ashley in Spanish. He said nothing, acting as if he didn't understand a word. When Ashley was asked if Dalton was her lover, he almost dropped his wallet. She vehemently denied it, insisting they were merely colleagues.

Dalton gave the waitress his widest smile, he dropped cash on the check, and said to both women, "Ella podría hacer peor."

The waitress laughed. "Yes, sir. She could do a lot worse."

He followed a silent Ashley to his rental, slid behind the wheel, and fastened his safety belt. "Where to?"

"Take a left at the next light." She buckled her seat belt. "You could have told me you spoke Spanish."

"It's in my file."

"I didn't get that far."

"You could have told me about the salsa," he countered.

"That was for staring at my ass in the parking lot."

"Then it was worth the burn."

Dalton drove to his hotel, checked in, and returned to his rental where Ashely waited. He was glad he'd left the car running. The air conditioning kept her from sitting in the heat. "I'm sorry it took so long. There was a couple ahead of me."

"Take a right out at the end of the drive and left at the second red light. The morgue is about five miles. You'll see the building on the right."

Dalton turned into the parking lot of a long white stucco structure with Servicio Medico Forense painted on the front. Six blue vans that needed a paint job were parked in front of the building. He drove into a slot one row behind them and killed the engine.

"We're early," Ashley said.

"So we are." He had no doubt she was going to grill him so he braced for it.

"You said you'd only met Ashton once?"

"Yeah, but I've never heard him called him that."

"Ashton Hilton Hunter."

"The name doesn't go with his reputation."

"Which is?"

"That Ash is a cold-blooded bastard."

She shrugged. "Only when he's pissed."

"That description fits a lot of people."

"Tell me about this Lost and Found Company you work for."

"It started with three college buddies who came together to help an old girlfriend who'd been kidnapped and sold to a sadistic bastard. There was a fourth friend, but he's on a ranch raising cattle. The business has grown over the last few years. When I first met them, they were working out of an office in a strip mall. Since then, the company has grown and has a state-of-the-art compound outside Dallas that would make Quantico jealous."

"I doubt that."

"You haven't been there. Trust me."

"That's not so easy for me to do."

"That attitude might keep you alive."

Rod Nunez drove onto the parking lot. Hopefully, that would put an end to their conversation. Except, Rod exited his car and shook his head.

Dalton nodded at Rod. "He's going in first."

"How long have you known him?"

"You are full of questions." She wasn't going to stop, so Dalton explained his friendship with Rod. "We were in the same unit for three years. He left the military and moved to his family's country. End of story."

Rod stepped out of the building and motioned for them to join him. Dalton got out but waited for Ashley at the hood of the car. "Have you ever been inside a morgue?"

"No. Don't worry about me, I'll be fine."

"You're sure?" Dalton wrapped his hand around her arm. Her muscle tensed and he released her.

"I'm sure."

He studied his fingers as she walked away. He needed to see if the sparks that had jumped between them were visible. If she'd felt anything, she hadn't blinked an eye.

Also By Jerrie Alexander
Romantic Suspense

The Green-Eyed Doll
The Last Execution
Hell or High Water
Cold Day in Hell
No Chance in Hell
No Greater Hell
A Helluva Holiday
Till Justice is Served
Till the Dead Speak
Someone To Watch Over Me
Flirting With Fate
Skyway to Hell – coming soon

Contemporary Erotic Romance

Come Hard
Come Hot
Come Together
Come Undone

Meet Jerrie

A career in logistics offered me the opportunity to travel to many beautiful locations in America, and I revisit them in her romantic suspense novels.

I write romantic suspense and contemporary erotic romance with alpha males and kick-ass women who weave their way through life's obstacles to emerge stronger because of, and on occasion in spite of, their love for each other. I like to put my characters in difficult positions, make them suffer, and if they're strong enough, they live happily ever after.

My books are written as standalone with no cliffhangers.

About the Author

A student of creative writing in her youth, Jerrie set aside her passion when life presented her with a John Wayne husband and a wonderful daughter. Her love for romantic suspense inspires her to write alpha males and kick-ass women. Her characters weave their way through death and danger to emerge stronger, because of, and on occasion, in spite of, their love for each other. If they're tough enough, they live happily ever after.

Jerrie lives in Texas, denies having an accent, thrives on sunshine, children's laughter, sugar (human and granulated), and researching for her heroes and heroines. She loves to hear from her readers. Find a complete list of her books at http://www.jerriealexander.com or contact her at jerrie@jerriealexander.com.

Read more at www.jerriealexander.com.

www.ingramcontent.com/pod-product-compliance
Lightning Source LLC
Chambersburg PA
CBHW051836130726
47987CB00002B/565